Everlight Tales
Short Story
Collection

Tiffany Shand

ACKNOWLEDGMENTS

Cover Design by Fenix Designs

Hunted Guardian

CHAPTER 1

Tyres screeched and Melanie Greenwood gripped onto the car's door handle for dear life. *Dear God, we are going to die if she keeps driving like this.* She was glad her gran had recommended locking the door after they had left their latest rental house in a hurry.

Her grandmother swung their battered little Honda Civic around the corner and light flashed by the windows. Mel could have sworn she had felt the tyres lift off the ground for a few seconds.

"Gran, you'll crash the car if you're not careful," Mel grumbled, and brushed her long curly brown hair off her face. "Please slow down. You don't need to drive like a maniac." She still didn't know why they had left the house in such a hurry. One moment everything had seemed normal when they had come home from late night shopping, but then gran had insisted they needed to leave at once.

"We've got to keep moving." Her gran swerved again, and horns blared as other cars almost collided into them. She didn't sound the least bit flustered. Mel wondered how she managed to keep her cool. "I told you to keep your head down. Why do you never listen to me?"

She didn't want or need to keep her head down. This was just another one of her grandmother's episodes. Mel didn't bother answering the question. "You'll get us killed if you keep driving so bad."

How she wished she had managed to find a doctor who could give her gran some help. But Gran never let her go near a GP surgery. Mel had never been sick a day in her life either, so pretending to be hadn't convinced Gran to take her to see a doctor. Her gran needed help and after tonight she would make sure she got some.

Her gran ignored her.

Mel glanced behind them. As usual, she saw nothing except a black mass darting alongside them in the shadows. She had seen it so many times, but her gran had never told her about what it was or why it kept following them. Mel decided it was just a shadow. What else could it be? She didn't share her grandmother's paranoia nor would she take part in her delusions.

She pushed her long hair off her face once more and stared at herself in the rising mirror. Her pale skin looked ghostly in the dancing city lights and her blue eyes had dark circles under them. Her grandmother looked just as dishevelled with her weathered skin, messy long grey hair that she had swept back in a bun and washed-out blue eyes.

Mel prayed they wouldn't crash. Most of her life had been spent running, never staying in one place for too long. Whenever Mel asked her gran about it, she either got ignored or Gran made up some excuse. All Gran had told her was it was important for them to keep moving.

Melanie was sick of the excuses and the needless running. But she couldn't demand answers right now. Not the middle of a high-speed chase. If she distracted her grandmother too much things were going to get very bad.

Lights blurred past as Gran swerved and sped around the unfamiliar city streets. The glowing lights and towering buildings felt so alien to her after leaving their house in the woods.

Melanie still had no idea where they were. Usually, whenever they moved somewhere they stayed in rural areas in the middle of nowhere with nothing but trees for company.

"Where are we going?" Mel asked instead. Perhaps that would be something her gran would answer.

"Somewhere safe," was all Gran said.

Mel sighed. Where was safe? Every time they moved Gran insisted it would be safe. Mel had liked the new house, and everything had seemed fine until they had come home from shopping and Gran had freaked out over something. Mel couldn't remember what it had been or what had caused it. Everything had still looked the same to her when they had walked in.

She sometimes wondered if the so-called danger was all in her gran's head. People had mental illnesses – she'd read about them in the hope she might find out if Gran had one. Bringing up the possibility of seeing a doctor hadn't gone over well with Gran.

Maybe I'm paranoid too and I'm imagining that shadow thing. Mel turned around again, and a sliver of fear ran down her spine. *What is it and why does it keep chasing us?*

The shadow darted along from building to building, blacking out the bright lights.

People could hallucinate when they were scared, couldn't they?

An old woman with a rollator was crossing the road and screamed as their car veered towards her.

"Gran, watch out! You're going to run her over!" Mel shut her eyes and braced herself for the inevitable impact.

It didn't come. Cars swerved and more horns blared.

Please let this be over soon.

"Gran, you're going to get us killed. Slow down!" Mel opened her eyes again and reached across the seat to grip her grandmother's arm. "Maybe we should head to the hospital."

Her grandmother gave a harsh laugh. "Why would we need to go to hospital? Neither of us is hurt yet."

"No, but you're not right in the head," Mel wanted to say. The words were there on the edge of her tongue, but she couldn't voice them out loud. Not yet. It was best not to start an argument at a time like this.

Gran turned the wheel as the shadow darted in front of them.

Gran said some strange words Mel couldn't quite make out. Energy vibrated through the air and glass exploded outward, static humming against Mel's skin. The car swerved again and collided with something solid. Light exploded around them and the car flipped over. Once, twice, three times. Blood roared through her ears.

Mel screamed; her head spun from the violent impact. The spinning seemed to go on forever as the car continued to flip over.

Mel kept her eyes shut. She knew death was coming. Its icy fingers reached out for her. She was too young to die at only seventeen. She hadn't even begun to live yet.

Why hadn't she done more to get her grandmother help with her mental illness? Why hadn't she demanded more answers? Thoughts raced through her whirling mind as the car continued its nerve-wracking spiral.

Maybe in death, she would get answers to all of her questions. Maybe her gran would at least find some peace then. At least they won't have to run anymore, she tried to tell herself as tears filled her eyes.

It wasn't enough. Mel wasn't ready to die yet.

Finally, the car stopped, turning the right way up.

Mel held her breath for several moments and waited. Death's icy touch retreated, and her heart pounded in her ears like a jackhammer. She took several deep breaths, gasping for air. Mel couldn't believe it. She was still alive. Her seatbelt dug into her neck like the edge of a knife.

Mel felt around her body, relieved to find she was still in one piece. Her ears rang so loud it took a few moments for her to hear her gran speaking.

Her vision swam, and she had to blink a few times. Slowly the world came back into focus. The bright lights stung her eyes and the onslaught of racing cars in city noise screeched through her ears.

"Melanie, are you alright?" Gran asked.

"I…think so." Mel blinked a few times. "Are you okay?" She looked her grandmother up and down. At least they both seemed to be breathing and unharmed.

Gran drew a knife from somewhere and cut through her seatbelt. Her long grey-hair had fallen out of its bun and blood had splattered across her forehead. "I'm fine. We need to get out of here." Gran turned and sliced through Mel's seatbelt.

Mel glanced through the windscreen and gasped as the black mass of darkness moved towards them. It blocked out the array of shimmering city lights in the distance. "Oh God, what is that?"

Had she hit her head during the crash? Was she hallucinating now too? She touched her forehead, searching for any sign of a bump or a graze. But found none.

Gran grabbed hold of her arm and said some strange words again. Light spiralled around them. Mel squeezed her eyes shut and her head spun once more.

Mel gasped as she fell onto hard ground. She took several deep breaths. Hard dirt brushed against her face and cold air hit her like tiny knives.

The city lights, the car and that strange shadow thing had vanished.

Somehow they had ended up outside and the car had vanished. Trees surrounded them, staring at them like dark watchful spectres.

Mel drew in another breath then let it out as she scrambled up into a sitting position. "How… How did we get out of the car?" Mel rubbed her face and ran a hand through her hair. "We were trapped." She used her other hand to rub her eyes, half expecting this to be a dream or a hallucination like that shadow thing they had seen at the back of the car.

Gran leaned back against the tree and sighed. "It doesn't matter. We are safe for the moment."

Trees surrounded them on all sides. They were in a forest in the middle of nowhere. In the distance, the city lights shone like bright beacons.

They couldn't have moved from one place to another, though, could they? Not in a matter of seconds.

Mel had seen her gran do some strange things over the years. Teleporting hadn't been one of them. Had her grandmother somehow used this magic?

No, that made no sense. Sure, magic might exist in their world since the fae had saved their planet several years earlier. Mel had never learned much about the fae nor cared to do so. She had never even met one of the creatures of legend since they mostly kept to themselves or had retreated back into their own realm.

"We need to get moving." Gran stopped to catch her breath. "It will be searching for us again."

"What will?" Mel demanded. "What was that thing?" She put her hands on her hips. "I want answers. Right now. No more hiding the truth from me. You can't hide anything from me anymore. Not after what's happened tonight."

Gran sighed and shook her head. "We have to go. I promise I'll explain everything once we're safe. But right now, we don't have time to waste. If we don't get moving, that shadow will find us, and we will both die."

A sliver of fear ran down her spine, but Mel didn't weaken her resolve. "No. How the hell did we get out of the car and come here?"

"Melanie, you don't understand how dangerous that thing is." Gran tugged at her arm, but Mel stood firm. "Please, stop fighting me and just do as I say for once."

"You always promise to give me an explanation and never do," Mel snapped. "I deserve to know the truth. Was… Was that some kind of magic?"

The whole idea was ridiculous. She had always thought the idea about the fae saving the earth had been some kind of fairy tale. Sure, people might have saved the planet, but that didn't make the fae real. But then her grandmother had somehow found a way to teleport Mel. She didn't know how else to explain it.

Gran bit her lip. "It… Come on. It's close by. I can sense it." She grabbed Mel's arm and pulled. "We have to move. I'll carry you if I have to."

Mel scoffed at that. Being a woman in her late sixties, Mel knew full well her grandmother couldn't carry her anywhere. An iciness came over her — like she had felt back in the car and that shadow thing had chased them.

God, had it found them already? If so, how?

Gran gripped her arm and dragged her past several trees and Mel stumbled as she fought to get her arm loose. Her grandmother's grip was a lot stronger than she would have thought possible for an old woman.

Together they hurried through the woods. Mel was glad now she had thought to put on jeans and boots. It made the trek a little easier.

She wanted to stop and demand answers from Gran again but decided against it. Gran was right about one thing. Now wasn't the time, not with that thing after them. Once they got somewhere safe, she would damn well get answers whether Gran wanted to give them to her or not. The time for secrecy was over.

The icy feeling grew more intense. Then she spotted the black mass edging towards the trees behind them.

"Oh, crap." Mel's heart pounded in her ears. "How did it find us? What is it?"

"Go, Melanie." Gran gave her a shove. "Keep going until you get back into the city. I've called the Guardians. Trust no one but them."

Guardians? What Guardians? Mel had no idea what she was on about. Gran had never mentioned them before or who they might be. As far as she knew her grandmother was her legal guardian. Yet somehow she suspected that wasn't the kind of guardian Gran had been referring to.

Light flashed between her gran's hands and a sword appeared.

Mel gasped, unable to believe her eyes. Since when did her gran use a sword? The only weapon Mel had ever seen her wield was an old-fashioned broom.

What was her gran? And why hadn't she told Mel about any of this craziness before now?

She had no idea what any of this meant. Her mind raced with confusion and dozens of unanswered questions.

The blackness came closer and two beasts shot out of the darkness. They were canine-like with fangs and hairy bodies, yet they stood on two legs.

Gran leapt into action and swung the sword at the first beast as it came at her.

Mel stood there, frozen. This couldn't be real. Any moment now she would wake up from this nightmare and find herself back at the rental house in her new, uncomfortable bed and a tiny little bedroom she had planned on painting.

"Run, Melanie! Go!"

The second beast came straight towards Mel.

Mel turned and ran, her boots clunking against the hard ground. She wished she had a weapon on her. A knife. Something she could use to defend herself with, but she had nothing. The only choice she had now was to keep running.

She hated leaving Gran behind, but at least she seemed to be able to take care of herself. Heck, she had a sword to fight with, and she seemed to know how to use it.

Mel wanted to gag at the stench of the creature's foul breath. She yelped as her foot got caught in a tree branch. Mel stumbled, but managed to regain her footing. She spun around and saw the beast was almost upon her.

God, I'm going to die. Mel took off running again then hit the ground as her foot caught on something. Pain exploded inside her ankle. She didn't know if it was broken or just sprained.

She raised her hands to shield herself as the beast leapt at her. Light flared around her palms, forming a shield of glowing pink light. It knocked the beast away from her.

Mel stared at her hands in disbelief.

"Hey!" A dark-haired man and blond-haired woman appeared from the tree line.

Where did these strangers come from? What were they doing here?

The beast charged towards them.

In one swift move, the man cut off the beast's head.

The woman rushed over to Mel. "Are you okay?"

Mel continued to stare at her hands as the light she had seen faded from them.

Had she just used magic?

CHAPTER 2

"Are you hurt?" The woman kneeling beside her gave her a concerned look. She had long blond hair, pale skin and blue eyes. She wore a dark blue jacket and black jeans along with a sword strapped across her back. "Are you Melanie? It's okay, we're not here to hurt you."

Mel blinked, still fixated on her hands. They had stopped glowing.

Had she imagined it? What had that strange light been? It couldn't have come from her. She could barely use a microwave. How the heck could she throw light from her hands? This whole night had been nothing but a series of random craziness. None of it made sense.

"Melanie?" She flinched when the woman put her hand on her shoulder. "Are you hurt?"

The man came over. He had short, curly black hair and grey eyes. "The beast is gone. The other one disappeared. Is she okay?

"What... What happened?" Mel finally found her voice and lowered her hands. She had to have imagined that strange light. If she had some kind of freaky magic, she would have known about it long before now.

"You were attacked by lycans but it's okay. You're safe

now," the woman said. "I'm Jess—"

Mel scrambled up. "Where's my gran?" She hadn't run that far before she'd fallen. "Gran?" she called out her.

Her gran wasn't anywhere to be seen. Ignoring her throbbing ankle, she trudged off. Her grandmother had to be around there somewhere. You can't disappear into thin air. Then Mel remembered how Gran had teleported them out of the car earlier. Okay, so maybe she could, but she wouldn't leave Mel behind. That was one thing Mel was certain about, despite all the weird stuff that happened that night.

"Melanie, wait." Jess moved in front of her. "Your grandmother called us to help you. We are Guardians. I'm Jess Monroe and this is my brother, Simon."

Mel stumbled and yelped from the pain in her ankle.

"Whoa, there." Simon put a hand out to stop her. "You're doing more damage to it if you keep moving."

"But my gran – I have to find her."

Her gran had been at the bottom of the hill. Damn it, she needed to get down there. In a blur of movement, she found herself in the spot she had just been thinking about.

Her head spun and her stomach recoiled at the sensation. How had she got down there so fast? Why did all these strange things keep happening to her?

This had to be a nightmare. One she wanted to wake up from right now.

Mel waited, half expecting herself to do just that.

Nothing happened.

"Gran?" she called out again. "Gran, where are you? Answer me."

This was the last spot she'd seen her in. All that remained was the sword Gran had been using.

Jess and Simon hurried downhill. Mel bent and picked up the sword. It shimmered with strange symbols along its hilt and felt heavy in her hand. Yet it was real nonetheless. Proof that this hadn't been some freaky nightmare.

Had her gran disappeared too? If so, why? Mel

somehow doubted Gran would have left her sword behind.

"That weapon belonged to the Guardian," Simon remarked.

"I don't know what that is." Mel shook her head.

None of this made any sense to her. It was too bizarre to be real. Yet the weight of the sword in her hand felt real enough.

More questions raced through her mind, but she knew she wouldn't get any real answers. Not unless she found her grandmother first. Why had her gran called these people to help? Who were they and why would they help her? They were strangers. She had never seen them before in her life. Gran had always told her to never trust strangers or talk to anyone. It had made for a lonely existence growing up, and she had never even had the chance to attend school like a normal teenager.

Instead, Gran had home-schooled her and insisted they didn't need anyone else. They moved around a lot because they enjoyed the adventure. At least that was what Gran had said in the beginning. Mel had never liked moving around and would have been happier settling in one place for once. Now she wondered if she would ever get the chance to see her grandmother again. Or to find out the truth from her.

"Guardians are supernatural beings. We keep miscreant fae in line and protect humans from them," Jess explained. "We were called by Slantra to come and get you. She told us it was urgent and begged us for help. We got here as soon as we could."

"Was that your grandmother?" Simon wanted to know. "You are Melanie, aren't you?" He eyed her up and down.

Mel hesitated. She didn't know these people. Although they had killed that beast and saved her life in the process. She didn't know whether to thank them for their help or to run away. What kind of people went around carrying swords?

"Find the Guardians," Gran had said. "They will help you. Trust no one but them."

If only she had had the chance to ask what that had meant. To get some real answers from her grandmother. But there was no point in dwelling on that now. All that mattered was finding her gran again. Answers would have to wait until later. Mel didn't have any idea on where to even begin looking or what to do next.

"I don't know who Slantra is." She gripped the sword tighter. "Yes, I'm Mel. Where's my gran?"

"The other lycan must have taken her," Simon answered.

Mel gasped. The idea of one of those awful creatures dragging her grandmother away terrified her and made her blood run cold. "I have to find my gran. Where do I find the lycan?" She shook her head. The question sounded so ridiculous.

Lycans weren't real. They were strange creatures that belonged in films.

"We'll take you somewhere safe. Don't worry, we won't leave you out here in the cold with nowhere to go." Jess put a hand on her shoulder. "Slantra used different names, like Penny Fairwin."

"Penny Fairfax is my gran. What are lycans?"

"A breed of shape-shifting fae who turn out every full moon," Simon explained. "We've been tracking them for weeks. It's a good thing we finally caught up with them."

"Where have they taken my gran?" Tears stung her eyes. No, she wouldn't have a meltdown. Falling apart and turning into a blubbering idiot wouldn't help her right now.

"We don't know if the lycan took her. Maybe she left to get to safety," Jess said. "Simon will search around here but I have to get you somewhere safe."

Mel opened her mouth to protest. She didn't want to leave. She wanted to look around and find her gran for herself. There was a chance Gran was still around here somewhere. She might be hurt, or worse... No, Mel wouldn't consider the possibility of her grandmother being gone. Gran was the only family she had, and she wouldn't lose her no matter what.

"Your gran asked us to help. You need that ankle looked at before you cause more damage to it. I can carry you back to my house," Jess said. "You'll be safe there and if your grandmother is still here Simon will find her. I'm sure she'll be fine."

Mel gaped at her. "How?" Judging by Jess' petite frame she didn't look like she could carry a bag of potatoes, let alone a lanky teenage girl. Yet her grandmother had used incredible strength earlier. Mel had felt it in her grip.

"I'm a Guardian. We have abilities of strength and speed." Jess gave her a reassuring smile. "I won't hurt you, Melanie. Slantra wanted us to help you, and we will."

Mel hesitated then reluctantly nodded.

Jess picked her up and shot away.

Mel bit back a scream and held onto the sword for dear life. Lights and colours blurred by in a whirlwind. Her stomach did uncomfortable flip-flops at the strange whizzing sensation. How is this even possible? People couldn't move at such speed. Then again, she suspected Jess wasn't a normal person. Or at least not human.

What were Guardians anyway? They had mentioned something about the fae. Mel still didn't understand what they were or where the hell they had come from.

They reappeared a few moments later outside a small house with a brown front door and dirty white-washed walls. There was light on the porch, but the rest of the house was in darkness.

Mel gulped as Jess set her back on her feet.

Jess opened the front door and motioned for Mel to follow. "Come in."

Mel followed her in.

The hallway was empty except for a couple of boxes. The walls were the colour of milky coffee and bear of anything. No pictures, no shoes scattered anywhere. Nothing. It didn't bother her too much though. She was so used to moving around and into houses that didn't have much in them. Sometimes Gran got lucky and managed to rent somewhere furnished but most of the time they had nothing except a few boxes of the bare essential items they needed like sleeping bags and toiletries. The rest they bought from local shops and made do with what they had.

"We haven't lived here for long," Jess said. "As Guardians we move around a lot."

Mel shook her head. "This is so… Weird."

"You didn't realise Slantra was a Guardian?" Jess arched an eyebrow. "I suppose she thought it was for the best."

There are so many things she had known about her grandmother. Had anything Gran told her been true?

"Why would my gran call you? How could she have disappeared?" Mel rambled. "I need to find her!" She resisted the urge to hurry back out the front door. If that strange speed thing appeared again maybe she would be able to get back to the woods and start searching for Gran herself. The idea filled her with hope, yet her throbbing ankle ached at the idea.

"Calm down. I'm sure your grandmother is fine." Jess turned on a light to reveal a small kitchen.

The cabinets were all dark wood, and chequered tiles covered one side of the wall. This place felt empty and un-lived in like many of the houses Mel and her gran stayed in.

"We don't know if she was taken. She might have teleported herself somewhere to get to safety," Jess remarked. "I wouldn't worry. She's a tough old bird. She will be fine. Slantra is legendary as a Guardian. She even fought in one of the fae wars."

Mel slumped into a chair at some table. "This is also unreal. I don't understand any of it."

"Guardians keep miscreant fae in line – didn't your

gran tell you anything about what we are? Or what we do?" Jess turned on a kettle.

Mel shook her head again. "No. I've never heard of Guardians or seen her…" Realisation dawned on her. All of those strange things her gran had done like setting crystals around or drawing strange marks around doorways. Now they made sense. "If she's a Guardian, what am I?"

She had not wanted to consider the possibility she might not be human. Yet that looked less likely to be true after everything she had seen tonight. Her mind flashed back to that strange light she had used earlier. It had felt good being able to protect herself like that, exhilarating in a way. Yet it also terrified another part of her. A part that didn't want to believe she wasn't human.

Jess brewed some tea and handed her a mug of it. "You're a Guardian too. How else could you move with supernatural speed and throw light from your hands? That was very impressive, by the way."

The back door banged open and Simon came in.

Mel shot to her feet, ignoring the throbbing in her ankle. "Did you find her?" Hope blossomed in her chest. She glanced behind him, half expecting to see her grandmother's familiar weathered face staring back at her. There was no one there.

She needed to get to her gran and make sure she was okay. Then she could ask her all the questions she had racing through her mind.

Only her grandmother had all the answers she needed. Not these strangers. They seemed nice enough, but she didn't want to stay here with them. She had never stayed with anyone else before. Gran might have said to trust them, but she still didn't know if she could.

Simon hesitated. "There wasn't any sign of her. I'm sorry. We'll go out and search again at first light."

Mel slumped onto the chair and put her head in her hands. "I-I need to call the police and report her missing."

Simon gave a harsh laugh. "The police can't do anything. It would be pointless in calling them. They're not equipped to deal with something like this. They don't even know anything about Guardians."

"I have to do something," Mel snapped. "They could help me find her."

"How would you explain about the lycans and the magic? Humans don't know that much about the supernatural world. They may think they know everything about the fae but they don't. They'll think you're mad if you go to them and ask for help. Even if you did, there's nothing they could do. You would only be putting innocent lives at risk."

Her shoulders slumped. He had a point.

How could she explain about the things that happened? She didn't understand any of it herself.

The humans might know about the fae after they had saved the planet but most of the fae had retreated into their own realm and different areas on earth. Most people didn't pay much attention to the fae now.

It still didn't make sense. Her whole life had been a lie. She wondered if she really knew her grandmother at all.

Jess got to work and checked Mel's ankle. She said it was sprained but not broken.

"How long did those lycans chase you for?" Simon asked as he set the table with her.

Mel shrugged. "We've been running my whole life. We never stay in one place for too long either." She gripped her mug of lukewarm tea. "What else do you know about my gran?"

"Not much – aside from you and her there are no other Guardians left apart from us," Simon admitted. "We knew Slantra had been in hiding for years. Ever since her daughter was killed about sixteen years ago."

Mel's mouth fell open. "What? My mum died in a car accident when I was a baby." She put her head in her hands.

Had that been another lie? Was anything about her life true?

Everything her gran had ever told her now might not be true. Even what happened when her mother had died. Gran had never spoken about her daughter's death other than to say it had a bad car accident, and she had loved Mel very much. Her father had never been in the picture and Gran had insisted she hadn't even known who he was.

"How – how did my mother die?" Mel asked after a few moments.

Jess and Simon shared a glance. "The Unseelie King ordered all Guardians to be killed. He viewed us as a threat when one of us went dark a few decades ago. After that, we were killed off or we went into hiding."

Mel shook her head. "This is all so surreal."

"You've heard about how the fae came to earth after the humans destroyed their realm, haven't you?" Jess asked.

She nodded. "Yes, but sometimes I wondered if any of it was really true. I have never seen a fae before and people don't talk about them much nowadays."

"Fae is a general term. Humans think of them as fairies — some are, but there are hundreds of different kinds of fae. A lot of the bad ones were banished a century ago, but some still walk the earth," Jess explained.

All this new information made her head spin. But one thing still bothered her. "I... I don't have anywhere to go. Gran's car crashed last night after we were chased, and I never had a chance to go back to retrieve anything."

Jess smiled. "You'll stay with us, of course."

"What chased you?" Simon leaned back against the kitchen counter and crossed his arms.

"Something dark. A big shadow thing – is that the lycans?" She didn't want to remember those awful beasts or imagine what they might have done with her grandmother.

Simon shook his head. "No, there must be something

else. Lycans are shifters. They don't have that kind of power and it wouldn't have taken them years to find their prey."

"The best way to deal with this is to learn to control your powers." Jess put a hand on her shoulder. "It's the only way you'll be safe."

"How do I do that?"

"We'll teach you," Simon said. "Then we'll find out what is after you."

CHAPTER 3

Jess showed Mel up to a small spare bedroom upstairs. It had little more than a bed and a chest of drawers. Its beige and threadbare carpet were just as neglected as the rest of the house. She didn't get to see any more of the house, but Jess showed her where the bathroom was.

Mel cleaned up and slumped onto the bed. Its mattress felt hard and lumpy, but she had slept in worse places than this. Whenever she moved, she was often lucky to have a bed at all. Despite her whirlwind of emotions, she fell into an uneasy sleep.

Mel soon found herself back in the woods. Shadows danced around her, their eyes watching her every move as she ran. Something was chasing her again, its hot breath on the back of her neck.

She had to run, had to find somewhere safe.

"Gran, where are you?" Mel called out.

She turned in every direction, searching for any sign of her grandmother, and found nothing but shadows. She tripped, her foot catching on something on the ground. She looked down; her gran stared up at her through glassy eyes.

"Melanie, you are in great danger. You must find the

Guardians before it's too late. Only they can teach you about your powers now."

"Gran? Where are you?" Mel reached out a hand to touch her yet somehow couldn't move forward to make contact with her grandmother. "I promise I'll find you."

"It's too late for me. You must worry about yourself now. Be safe, learn to control your power. Find the Guardians…" Gran looked away. "I wish I could have told you everything…"

"I've already found them. They promised they're going to help me find you. Where are you? Tell me you're okay." Tears stung her eyes.

"Find the Guardians…" Her gran's voice faded away and her body disappeared into the blackness.

Mel awoke with a jolt as slivers of light came in through the uncovered window. The remnants of the nightmare still flashed through her mind. The dream had felt so real. Almost as if her gran had been right in front of her. Her chest ached and she bit back a sob.

It took a few moments to realise this wasn't her room at the new rental house. That room had had hideous yellow wallpaper with flowers on it. She remembered how she had planned on painting the room. She had even bought the paint on her last shopping trip with her gran.

This wasn't the first time this had happened. They moved around so much it always took a while to get used to a place. Heck, she didn't even know how long she would get to stay here either. She couldn't expect Simon and Jess to house her forever. *What do I do?* She and her gran had never discussed what would happen to her if Gran died or went missing.

Since she was underage, she guessed she might have to go into foster care. Mel shuddered at that idea. She didn't want to live with complete strangers. All she wanted was to have her gran back and go back to their lives as they were. Even if it meant running around moving from one place to another again. At least they had had each other. That was all that mattered.

Mel scrambled up and everything from the night before crashed down on her.

Gran was missing and she was stuck with two strangers. She had nothing left. What little she had owned had been left behind in the car when it crashed. It was still dark out, so she must have only slept for a few hours.

She still couldn't believe it. Gran was gone and someone had had her mother killed.

Her chest grew tight. She couldn't breathe. She fumbled around, expecting to find a lamp, but there wasn't one.

Mel took in several heaving breaths as she stumbled out of bed and hurried to the door. She opened her mouth to call for help but couldn't form the words.

Simon had given her an old T-shirt to wear that fell to her knees. Jess' clothes had all been too small since Mel stood a head taller than her. Mel staggered downstairs. She needed air, needed to breathe.

Bright light crackled over her palms. Oh God, what was happening now? Why couldn't she breathe?

Mel hurried down the hall and out the open back door. Cold air hit her face like tiny needles. She took in deep lungfuls of air, but it didn't feel like enough.

Mel collapsed to her knees against the hard-concrete covering the back garden. She lay there and more static passed over her body.

What's happening to me? Why is this happening? Fear twisted in her stomach like a tight knot. She wished her grandmother was here. Maybe she could explain why all of this was happening. What it all meant.

Mel curled up in a foetal position as the pain grew more intense.

"Melanie?" someone called out her name.

It sounded far away somehow, but she couldn't open her mouth to respond. Not even if she wanted to.

Tears stung her eyes as she whimpered. Was she dying? It felt like she might be. Mel wanted the pain to go away, to end.

Simon knelt beside her.

"What's... Happening?" She rasped.

"Your powers must be emerging. Slantra must have bound them to keep you safe. You being in danger could have triggered them." Simon took hold of her hand. "It's okay. Just relax and let it happen. I'll be right here with you. There's nothing to be afraid of."

Mel squeezed her eyes shut and gripped his hand so tight she thought the bones might break. The pain seemed to go on forever.

After a while it finally subsided, and she could breathe again.

The light crackling over her palms faded too.

Simon still held onto her hand. His touch felt almost comforting. "See, I told you it would be okay. It's always frightening when a Guardian's powers first emerge. Especially if you haven't grown up with them."

The concrete felt rough and cold against her cheek. Where did the pain go? It didn't matter. She just felt relieved it was finally all gone and prayed it wouldn't ever come back again.

Mel shook her head. "This is all so crazy."

"I know, but that doesn't make it any less true. You have to learn to control your new powers if you want to save your gran and find out who is after you."

Mel scrambled up into a sitting position and pushed her long hair off her face. "I'll do whatever it takes to find my grandmother." But deep down, she didn't know if she wanted to be a Guardian.

"Come inside, I will make you breakfast, and we can get started with your training."

Jess disappeared later that morning, saying she would have a look around the woods for Melanie's gran. Mel had

24

wanted to go with her, but Jess had said it would be safer for her to stay at the house. Her ankle didn't feel so bad this morning, so that was one good thing at least. That didn't surprise her. She had always been a fast healer.

Simon led Mel outside into the back garden. It had a large paved courtyard and the rest was nothing but open woodland. Her gran would have loved a place like this. It was just the kind of place they always stayed in. Right in the middle of nowhere with no neighbours around and difficult to find. "Most Guardians usually have an active power. All Guardians have strength and supernatural speed. Like you used last night. Let's start with that."

"So aside from tracking down fae, what do Guardians do?" Mel asked. "Other than hide from whoever wants to kill them?"

Simon shrugged. "We lead normal lives like everyone else. We do what we can for work. Jess works at a local McDonald's and I do odd jobs around the nearby town as a handyman. We blend in just like any other humans would."

Mel refrained from mentioning the fact they weren't humans. Not really. She didn't want to offend him, not after everything he had done for her. Mel guessed he was only a few years older than her. Maybe early twenties.

"You and your sister are the only ones left? Aside from me and my gran?" Mel still had trouble getting her head around the fact she was more than human too. Before last night nothing strange had ever really happened her. Sure, she had thought her gran was off her rocker and had a mental illness, but she never used magic before then.

Maybe last night would prove to be a nightmare and this would turn out to not be real. She wanted her gran back and to feel safe again.

Mel frowned at that. No, she had never truly felt safe. As a kid, she had been terrified of the strange shadow creature. Even though her grandmother had always assured her she would never let it harm her. As she had grown older, she decided it wasn't real had brushed it off as her gran's paranoia. If only that had been true.

"Yes, many Guardians were wiped out on one of us going dark. Her name was Elena McKenzie. She was bad. She recruited a lot of fae to her cause."

"What does Unseelie mean?" They'd mentioned that term last night, but she had no idea what it meant.

"It's a term used for dark fae. Seelie means light fae. Dark doesn't always mean evil, though."

Mel shuddered. She didn't want to think about evil beings and the stuff of nightmares like those lycans had been. "You said they had been banished somewhere, right?"

"Some of them yes. Some good fae was sent there too along with Guardians," Simon said. "The Unseelie king tricked another Guardian into doing it. Guardians can open portals and banish fae to the underworld. Or at least we used to be able to. Our powers have grown weak over the years." He sighed. "Try using your speed first."

"I don't know how." Mel hated feeling like an idiot. God, why hadn't gran taught her any of this stuff? She must have known Mel would need to use it one day.

"Concentrate on where you want to go. It's about desire and willpower. Will yourself to move and you will," Simon said. "Focus on one spot."

Mel hesitated. She wanted to find her grandmother more than anything. Too bad her speed couldn't just take her to her gran.

Her body blurred as she almost slammed into a garage.

Mel put her hands out against the door. Why had she ended up here? She had been thinking of her gran, not the garage. This was not the place she had wanted to go to.

"Careful." Simon laughed as he shot over to her using his own speed. "You might bump into something. Were you thinking about the garage?"

The garage looked bleak and had a dirty window on the side. Mel couldn't make out much inside, other than something large on the floor.

Simon put her hand on her shoulder and steered her away from there. "Let's test your strength next." He went to pick up a barrel and lifted it as if it weighed nothing. "Try one of these."

Mel walked around to her side of the barrel. She grunted as she tried to lift the heavy weight. "What is in these?"

"Compost. Perhaps your strength hasn't manifested yet. Concentrate."

Mel tugged at the barrel, but it refused to budge.

Simon rubbed his chin. "Maybe you need to trigger it like you did your speed last night. Do you have the sword you found?"

She nodded. She had the sword in her room but left it by the door. "I'll go and get it." Mel headed off back inside the house. There was still no sign of Jess around.

Mel hadn't been able to find a clock anywhere in the house, so she still didn't know what time it was. Why didn't these people have a clock? She hadn't even seen them using mobile phones either, which struck her as odd.

She watched Simon from the window. He turned and disappeared inside the garage.

Mel took the opportunity to look around. Simon had been with her since breakfast, and she hadn't had a chance to snoop yet.

She headed into the living room. Nothing in there but a battered leather settee. What kind of people didn't own a TV?"

Weird.

The rest of the room was bare. No table. No bookcases. No knick-knacks or photos to make it feel like a home. It was like they had moved in with nothing.

Mel and her gran didn't have much, but they both held onto a few sentimental items to make a place feel like home.

Next, she headed upstairs where there were four doors.

The bathroom, she knew, was sparse except for a couple of shampoo bottles, soap and toothbrushes. But aside from the spare room, she hadn't opened any of the other doors.

Mel hesitated. She knew she shouldn't sneak around.

These people had been nothing but nice to her. Still, curiosity proved hard to resist.

Mel turned the handle on the door. It turned but wouldn't open. Locked, she realised. Mel tried the other one. Locked too. If they had nothing here, why keep the rooms locked?

It all seemed weird to her.

Were they hiding something? Just because they were nice didn't mean they were trustworthy.

Damn it, she wanted to get inside and have a quick look. Light sparked between her fingers, and she turned the handle again. Something clicked and the door swung open.

Inside, a single bed stood on the far side of the room covered in messy sheets. Women's clothes were strewn across the scuffed wooden floor along with disused takeaway packets. Nothing out of the ordinary, so why the lock on the door?

Mel shut the door and headed towards what must be Simon's room.

Something blurred in front of her. It was Simon, carrying a sword. "Were you looking for something?" His expression remained unreadable, but she thought she caught a flash of anger in his eyes.

Crap. She should have known better than to be so nosy.

Mel yelped and took a step back. "I — I can't get the door to the spare room open." She knew the lie sounded pathetic, but she didn't know what else to say.

What could she say?

"Sorry, you caught me snooping." That wouldn't sound great.

What if he decided to throw her out? Then she would be left on the street with nowhere to go.

Since Mel didn't have a mobile phone here, she didn't know what had happened to her gran's car either. And hadn't been able to check the news or social media to see if it had been found.

The car still held her possessions — if they were still there.

Simon frowned and opened the other door. "The spare room is here. Come outside when you're ready." He then blurred away again.

Mel breathed a sigh of relief. God, she needed to stop snooping.

Even so, was he trying to hide something?

CHAPTER 4

Mel spent the next couple of days learning how to use a sword. Or at least she tried. Simon wanted to make sure she could use both her strength and her speed.

The speed was coming along, but her strength still hadn't manifested. The magic remained elusive too. Mel didn't understand the strange light thing she could do with her hands. The worst part was the nightmares she had been having the past few nights. She always woke up covered in sweat.

In every dream, her gran kept telling her to find Guardians. Jess had heard her screaming the night before and told her to stop worrying. It was only a dream despite how real it felt to her.

That night Jess and Simon wanted her to practice opening portals. They explained that was how Guardians banished fae to the underworld.

Mel's stomach twisted into knots as she headed out with them into the nearby forest that night. The sky hung over them like a heavy blanket, with not a cloud or star in sight. The blackness felt almost oppressive somehow. Mel would have been happier if they had gone somewhere more well-lit. But she knew they couldn't go somewhere with humans around because that would raise a lot of unwanted questions.

"Now, you need to stay focused," Simon told her. "You are only opening a portal for a few seconds."

"Me?" Mel gaped at them. "I thought you were going to do it first to show me how it works?" Her heart rate kicked up a gear.

No way was she ready for this. She had wanted to see them do it first and see how it worked for herself. She still had trouble getting her head around all of this, but she did believe she had magic now. She had felt and seen enough over the past few days to know that it was real.

"We told you. We don't have the power to open portals ourselves," Jessica said. "Our powers are weaker than yours — at least in that respect. But don't worry, we know you can do it. Slantra was one of the most powerful Guardians. Legend has it she was even there when they banished Elena McKenzie."

"You don't have anything to worry about. You'll only be opening the portal for a couple of seconds." Simon put a reassuring hand on her shoulder. "It's to show you how it works. Once you become more well-versed in your abilities you will be able to open and close portals as easy as anything." He snapped his fingers as if this was a piece of cake.

Mel gripped her grandmother's sword. Jess had been out more than once looking for Gran but kept insisting there was no trace of her. She hadn't found out anything about the car either. It looked like she might be stuck living with these people for a while. She didn't know whether to feel relieved or disappointed at that.

They had been nothing but nice to her, but she wanted to find her gran for herself and to... To what? To go back to her life as it had been before?

No, that would be impossible now. Even if Gran did come back, things would never be as they were before.

Mel didn't know how they could be.

"How is this going to help me find my gran?" she asked. "Do you think my gran has been dragged into the underworld?"

"It's a possibility. There are fae nobles with enough power to do such a thing." Simon crossed his arms. "We haven't been able to find her anywhere else. When she ran away, she might have retreated into the underworld as a place of protection, and perhaps got stuck there. That's why you need to know how to open and close portals."

"Everything will be fine, Melanie." Jess gave her an impatient smile. "All you have to do is cast the runes we showed you on the ground and let your magic do the rest."

Mel glanced at the glowing hilt of her grandmother's sword. It had strange symbols on it too. Runes, they had told her. Using the tip of the blade she drew the strange symbols on the ground within a circle.

Keeping the sword grasped in one hand, she used her free hand to access her magic. Nothing happened at first.

"Let the magic flow through you. It should feel as natural as breathing," Simon said, and his jaw clenched.

She knew both of them were impatient for her to get this right. She had to make it work. It might be the only way of finding her grandmother again.

Mel closed her eyes and took a deep breath. Static sizzled between her fingers as a strange glowing pinkish-purple light surged from her hand, igniting within the circle she had drawn. More energy flowed out of her, like a dam breaking to burst. She gasped and sank to her knees. Of all the things she had expected, she hadn't thought opening a portal would feel like this.

"It is supposed to be draining my energy?" she gasped.

"Yes, keep doing it. It's the only way it will work." Simon leaned forward; his expression eager.

Mel struggled to remain upright as more and more energy flowed out of her. A glowing portal of light appeared. Dozens of shadows moved beyond it.

"Guardian," the voices whispered at her. "You have

come to free us."

What? No, she wanted to scream. To deny it. The portal was only supposed to appear for a few seconds, yet somehow she knew minutes had passed since she had cast the circle.

"It's working. Mel, keep adding more power into the circle." Simon came over, bent and slashed the blade of her sword against her palm.

She yelped in alarm. "What the hell are you doing?"

"We need your blood for this to work." All reassurance had gone from Simon's face and his expression hardened.

"It's working. It's finally working!" Jess clapped her hands together in glee and a wicked smile spread across her face.

"The lycans deceive you, Guardian," one of the voices hissed at her. "They only want you to free us. Then we will feast on your blood."

No, this was wrong. Everything inside her screamed for her to stop. Somehow, she knew this wasn't the way to find her grandmother. They were using her to break through the barrier to the underworld. An impenetrable wall of energy lay just beyond the portal. Its energy felt as familiar to her as her own energy. Guardian magic. They had created the barrier and only one of them could get through it.

"No!" Mel clenched her fist in an attempt to stop the drops of blood from falling to the ground. "I won't do this."

Simon growled at her. All at once, his human form faded away as his body twisted and curved into one of the beasts like she had seen in the night her gran had disappeared. Jess's form changed too as they circled around her.

Lycans. They were lycans.

They had tricked her and pretended to be her protectors. Why hadn't she listened to that dream all along? Why had she believed them?

It didn't matter now. Mel knew she had to get out of here and close the portal before it's too late. Gripping the edge of her sword she gasped and wrenched her bleeding hand away, pulling her magic back with it. All at once, the portal vanished and the awful hissing voices faded along with it.

Mel rose and swung the sword as one of the lycans lunged towards her. "Stay back! She snarled. "Where is my gran? What have you done with her?" More light sparked in her free hand. Magic came easily now, no doubt reacting to her anger.

They had taken her gran away, she knew it. They deserved to pay. Mel dropped the sword and raised her hands – None of the anger and frustration came out, but a surge of power. Both lycans screamed as her power tore them apart.

Afterwards, her knees hit the ground, too exhausted to move. She wanted to cry and let grief take its full hold on her. Her gran was gone. They must have killed her. She should have known. Ever since that night, when she had first had the dream where her grandmother told her to get to safety.

Instead Mel got up and with sword still in hand she blurred back towards the Monroe's house. To her surprise, the lights were on upstairs and down. There was even a light on inside the dingy garage.

Mel dropped the sword and hurried towards it. A tall dark-haired man with piercing blue eyes came out carrying a dishevelled-looking old woman.

"Gran!" Mel grasped. "Oh my God, she's still alive?" She couldn't believe it. Her gran had been here the whole time. "Who are you? What are you doing here?" Gran's eyes were closed, and she had deep gashes over her face and arms.

"My name is Nick Trevelyan. I am a Guardian — unlike the imposters it appears you've been staying with. Don't worry, your gran will be alright. But she will need rest and time to recover. It looks like they tortured her — no doubt to get her to open a portal."

A pretty dark-haired woman with dark eyes and wearing a leather jacket came out of the house. "Are you Melanie? It's good to finally meet you. I'm Zoe Finn – it's a good thing we found you in time."

Mel shook her head. This felt even more surreal than everything else that had happened the past few days. But she sensed the truth in their words. They were true Guardians; she could feel it in their power.

"How did you find me?"

"We sensed your power. We tried to find you a few nights ago, but they vanished before we had a chance to get there and retrieve you," Zoe explained. "I'm sorry about your grandmother, but she's a tough old bird. If anyone can get through this, she can."

Mel followed the Guardians back inside the house and gave her gran a big hug. Her grandmother remained unconscious, but she was alive. They would have a lot to talk about when this was all over.

"What happens now?" Mel asked the Guardians. "Are people going to keep coming after me?"

Nick and Zoe glanced at each other. "We have been talking about that, and we think you should come to an academy where we work. It's for gifted students like you. You would be safe there, and maybe then we could figure out who is chasing you."

Mel frowned. "Are there more Guardians there?"

Nick shook his head. "No. Aside from you, your grandmother and us two. We are all that is left. But we would be happy to train you properly and to teach you what it means to be a Guardian."

"I'll think about it."

All she wanted now was for her gran to get better again, and to sleep for a year. Maybe then she could comprehend all the awful things that had happened and begin anew. And find out more about the academy they had mentioned.

THE END

Banshee's Revenge

CHAPTER 1

Insert chapter five text here. Insert chapter five text here. Lily Monroe stalked down the street, surprised not to see any trick or treaters around. Instead, the street remained eerily quiet. Nothing stood on either side of the road and a few lights shone from the large townhouses.

Weren't kids supposed to love Halloween? Or Samhain as it was really called? All of the kids that she worked with in foster care usually did.

Lily smiled to herself. She looked forward to a night with her coven. The veil between the worlds was always thinnest on this night. Lily and her coven would take advantage of that. Lily ran a hand through her long, dark pink hair as a chill ran over her. Halloween was supposed to be a creepy night, she reminded herself.

She picked up the pace and hurried further down the street.

Lily stopped. The silence struck her as strange. She lived in a busy town. Yet there was no drone of traffic, no rambling from people stumbling out of pubs. No kids going from house to house looking for sweets.

Why was it so quiet?

She pulled her leather jacket tighter and hurried further

down the road. In a couple of minutes, she would reach her higher priestess' house and be safe. Madge's house was warded, and they would be able to call to the other side in safety.

Get a grip, she told herself. *There's nothing to be afraid of.* She shivered again and ran. She didn't know why but everything inside her screamed at her to run. Her boot heels clicked on the pavement as she ran faster.

Mist swirled around her so thick and heavy it made the hairs on her arms stand on end. Lily sprinted until a bolt of lightning struck her. It surged through her back and cut through her chest. She gasped for breath but couldn't draw in any air.

She collapsed to the ground as the mist sucked her in. Darkness swallowed her and her heart stopped. Lily blinked and found herself staring down at her body. What the hell? No, she couldn't be dead.

That mist couldn't have killed her, could it?

"Wake up!" She screamed at her body.

She was too young to die. Lily had so much she wanted to do. What would happen to the foster kids she worked with? Her dream had always been to be a social worker and help others. She couldn't just walk away from that. Too many lives depended on her.

"Wake up!" She reached out to shake herself and her hands passed straight through her body.

"It's too late," a voice said from behind her.

Lily spun around to see a short, balding, overweight man standing there. "Who are you?" She frowned.

"I have a lot of names. In short, I am Death, but you can call me Grim."

Grim? The Grim Reaper was a short, bald bloke who looked like he belonged in McDonald's. Lily would have laughed if she hadn't been standing over her corpse. She turned and spotted a man run out of a nearby doorway. Judging by his clothes she recognised him as one of the street sleepers she often handed food out to. Goddess, had he seen her die? She knew he couldn't be her killer since he was a human.

"I don't understand. I can't be dead." She shook her head. "I don't even know how I…" She couldn't bring herself to say died. "… How I ended up like this."

"Someone conjured a portal and you ended up walking into it as it started materialising. Bad luck, Lily."

She narrowed her eyes. "You know my name?"

"Yes, I'm here to escort you into the next life. If that's what you want," Grim said. "You can find peace in the afterlife or stay here. It's your choice but you will be trapped in this plane forever if you stay."

Lily hesitated. She knew what happened to souls who remained earthbound. They walked around with no one except for a few supernaturals who were able to see and talk to them. She didn't want to have to endure that kind of lonely existence. Even if it meant she could stay here and watch over the people she cared about.

But hell, she was pissed off! What gave someone the right to kill her? She didn't want to walk around the afterlife in peace either. Her life had been stolen from her and she damn well deserved justice.

"I want to stay here," she said finally.

Grim raised his hand and a glowing portal disappeared. "It's your choice. I'll get going then. Halloween is a busy night for me."

"No, I want my life back." Lily crossed her arms.

Grim scoffed. "You're dead, sweetheart. Ain't no changing that."

Lily jumped back inside her body.

"That won't work either."

Lily sighed and stood up. "I'm not moving on and I'm not going to be a lost soul either. There must be a third option."

"There's one but it's not for the fainthearted. You could become an agent of death."

"You mean like you?" She arched her brow. Being a

witch, she knew about the Grim Reaper and a bit about the afterlife. But she didn't know how everything on the other side worked. That seemed like an unreasonable choice too. Why couldn't Grim just give her life back?

Grim laughed. "God no, there's only one grim and that's me. No, you'd be working for me as someone who escorts souls into the next life as a banshee. You'd get to see the world but like I said it ain't for the fainthearted."

Lily hesitated. Her life was over. Her life as a witch and a social worker at least. "Fine, I'll be the best damn banshee you've ever had."

One year later

Lily appeared inside a living room where the body of an old woman lay sprawled on the floor.

Heart attack. One of the perks about her job as a banshee was she knew how someone had died. This seemed a little more peaceful than her death had been. Hell, at least it was a natural way to go.

Now, where was the woman's spirit? It had to be floating around here somewhere.

"Nancy?" Lily called. "It's okay. I'm here to help you." Lily waited and picked at her nails.

She always gave people a warning when it was their time to go. So they could get their affairs in order. She sure as hell didn't screech in warning like some of the other banshees did either. Instead, she told people face-to-face. Not all of them believed her. Some went straight into denial or some tried to attack her. As if that would do any good. Lily wished people would just deal with it. Death was inevitable for everyone.

Lily had never seen the appeal of screeching either. Screeching would only scare the crap out of someone. Sure, not everyone took her warning seriously, but she stayed true to her word. She had become a damn good banshee and had the highest success rate out of all of them. More people chose to move on because of her.

Lily paced up and down, but no spirit appeared. She sighed and tapped her foot. "I guess we'll have to do this the hard way." She sighed and reached into the wall. In one move she pulled the spirit out. "There's no point in hiding from me."

The woman thrashed and kicked. "No, I'm not dying." There was always one who refused to go.

"Nancy, look. You're dead." Lily motioned to the body. "There's nothing keeping you here. I warned you this would happen."

Nancy, an elderly woman, wore a long nightgown and had her hair in rollers. She sighed. "My grandkids — they won't have anyone to watch out for them."

"They'll be fine. They wouldn't want you to be stuck here, would they?" Lily's expression softened. "Don't you want to see your husband and all your family on the other side? They'll be waiting for you."

Nancy hesitated. "They are?"

"Of course. They know it's your time."

Nancy gave her body one last glance then nodded.

Lily waved her hand and the portal opened. She and Nancy then stepped through.

After Lily had dropped Nancy off at the other side, she stepped back through the portal to go and find Grim. Since it was Halloween, she had a chance to take human form again and walk back on earth. But first, she had to get permission from Grim to do so. That made her laugh. Getting permission from him of all people. The dead were allowed to walk freely among the living today, so she didn't know why banshees had to ask first.

As she passed out from the other side something tugged at her. Light flashed around her and a voice echoed in arrears. Someone had cast a summoning spell to summon the spirit.

She heard the name Freya Goodwin being mentioned. Someone was trying to summon Freya's spirit.

Lily paused. Grim had warned her about Freya Goodwin.

Who would be trying to summon Freya? They were wasting their time anyway.

She was tempted to just ignore the call but decided to investigate. It wouldn't take her long to find out who it was and then she could be on her way to see Grim.

Lily reappeared in a room with blue walls and before her stood a pretty girl with long silvery blonde hair and blue eyes.

"Silvy." Lily smiled when she recognised the foster kid who she had once been a social worker to. Silvy had always been one of her favourite kids.

"Lily, is that you?" Silvy frowned. "Wait, are we blood-related?"

Lily snorted. "Hey, kid, and no we're not."

Silvy frowned. "Then why are you here? Wait, I heard you'd been killed a few months ago."

Lily winced. "I…was. Now I'm a banshee." She rolled her eyes. "Long story."

Silvy stepped away from her "You're not here to warn me about my death, are you?"

A laugh escaped Lily's mouth. "No, kid. Banshees don't just warn of death. We help to escort souls to the other side."

"I want to talk to Freya — my birth mum."

"That's why I've come. You can't see her, I'm sorry."

Silvy gaped at her. "Why not? This book says I can summon the spirit of anyone. I need to see her."

Lily hesitated. She couldn't tell Silvy the truth. Grim would obliterate her soul if she said anything.

"It's complicated."

"Then make it simple. I've lost her twice and I need to know things only she can tell me."

"I'm sorry, kid. I only came here to give you a heads up." Lily decided it was time to leave. She didn't have time to waste. She had to get Grim and get permission to go walking around in the human world. There were only a few hours left before midnight. After that, she would have to wait an entire year to search for her killer again. Smoke enveloped her body.

"Wait!" Silvy reached out and grabbed her arm.

To her amazement, Lily became solid once more. How had the kid done that?

"Whoa, how did you do that?"

"I've no idea. Please just tell me what you know. Why can't I see Freya?" She gave Lily a pleading look. "Forget the stupid rules. I need answers."

Lily felt a pang of guilt. She loved this kid but knew she couldn't break the rules for her.

"Silvy, I can't just break the rules for you like I did when you were a foster kid." Lily tugged at her arm but Silvy didn't loosen the grip. She looked around Silvy's room. She was in a much better place now. It was pointless for her to find Freya's spirit.

"I see you have moved up in the world." She commented.

"I need to talk to her and if she is a spirit, there's no reason why I can't do that." Silvy flinched sharply. "Whoa, someone killed you, didn't they? A warlock from the look of it." Silvy arch an eyebrow.

Lily's eyes widened. "How do you know that? What warlock? Tell me what you saw."

Silvy shook my head. "Why should I? You won't tell me why I can't see my birth mum."

Lily sighed. "You always were a sneaky kid, Silvy. I'm sorry, I can't tell you anything."

"Then you don't want to know anything about the warlock?" I arched an eyebrow at her. "Like maybe his name... Or where he is?"

Lily froze. "How could you know that?" She had always known Silvy was gifted and she had magic. Silvy had always denied having such a thing despite being half-fae.

"I have magic now — I think you've always suspected it. The only difference now is I'm starting to learn how to use it."

Lily shook her head again. "I can't break the rules for you as I used to when I was your social worker. You have no idea how much trouble I would get into. I wouldn't just lose my job. My soul would be at stake."

Silvy dropped her arm. "I can't give up on trying to find my mother. You know me well enough to know that."

Lily bit her lip and hesitated. If Grim found out about this her soul was toast. "I don't know where her spirit is, Silvy. I swear I don't. None of the banshees escorted her soul on to the other side."

Silvy gaped at her. "Then what happened to her? That makes no sense. All souls are supposed to pass on when they die, aren't they?"

"Sometimes yes. But other spirits choose to stay earthbound. Especially if they have unfinished business."

"Then how do I find her?"

Lily shook her head. "I have no idea. That's not part of my job description. Now tell me what you know about that warlock."

"He opened a portal which is what killed you. The portal opened up right in the spot where you were. His name is Jared, and he was in a house performing a ritual not far from where you were struck down. I swear that's all I know."

A warlock. Finally, she had an answer to one of her questions.

Lily grinned. "That's good enough." Lily sighed and shook her head. "I have to go. Don't try summoning her spirit again. It won't work." Lily vanished in a whoosh of smoke.

Lily reappeared outside Grim's office. She still found it hilarious to think Death had an office filled with piles of scattered paperwork.

Her thoughts raced with questions. Finally, she had an answer. And from one of her foster kids no less.

"Grim, it's Halloween today," Lily remarked. She still couldn't believe it had been an entire year since she had died. In that time, she learned everything she could about the other side and how things worked there.

Just because she was a banshee now didn't mean her desire to live again and get revenge on the bastard who had killed her had waned. Hell, it had only gotten stronger. Being a banshee meant she could still walk among humans for brief periods of time but it wasn't the same. Sure, she could go anywhere in the world, but she wasn't alive anymore. Not really.

Now her only role was escorting souls into the next life. Sometimes it felt good. Most of the time it sucked to see so many lives wiped out for no reason.

"You can't have the night off," Grim stated and leaned back in his chair. "You know it's one of our busiest times. I've got to work myself today too."

Lily waited, half expecting him to berate her for going and talking to Silvy. But he didn't look annoyed. Maybe luck was on her side today.

One thing she had learned about Grim — he much preferred being here to out there doing the job himself.

Lazy bugger. Lily put on her brightest smile. "Grim, you know I need revenge on the bastard who killed me."

"You are still on this revenge kick?" Grim rolled his eyes. "I thought you would be over that by now."

"Someone caused my death and took my entire life away." Her hands clenched into fists. "I deserve to get revenge."

"You have a good life. You get to walk among humans all over the planet."

"Grim, I know I can walk free on Halloween. I just need the chance to find my killer," she said. "I'm not waiting another year."

"What good will revenge do you? It won't give you

your old life back."

"I still need to know why he did what he did. What the reason was." She put her hands on her hips. "I just got a lead. I know it was a warlock. Just give me the chance to find out who he is and talk to him."

Grim sighed. "It's always about reasons with you. Sometimes there is no reason."

"Everything happens for a reason." That much she had learnt during the past year. "Please just give me this one chance."

Grim groaned. "Fine. You have the next few hours to find the killer. But you know the rules — you can't use your powers to take his life."

"I won't use my powers," she promised.

No, she didn't need her powers to hurt him. There were other ways of doing that.

CHAPTER 3

Lily and Jared reappeared in a graveyard a few miles away.

Jared gasped as he almost fell over. "Where... Where are we?"

"Someplace safe."

"A graveyard?" Jared's eyes went wide. "Why did you bring me here? Are you going to kill me? Why didn't you just let that demon finish me off?"

"Because I have questions, and no one is going to kill you. At least not here on holy ground."

Grim would obliterate herself if she dared to violate such a rule. She wanted revenge but she wasn't an idiot.

"I'm sorry for what happened to you," Jared said. "I really am. Please believe me when I say I never meant for it to happen."

"You think an apology is going to make it all better?" She snarled. "You took my life. No apology will ever be enough to make up for that." Lily put her hands on her hips. "I brought you some time by bringing you here. The demon can't step foot on holy ground, much less harm anyone here."

"There's nothing else I can tell you. Taking my life

won't give you yours back, will it?"

"Something tells me you're too much of a coward to trade your life for mine anyway. Which would be the right thing to do."

"Listen, lady, I'm sorry you got caught in the crossfire but all due respect you look pretty alive to me," Jared snapped back.

"That's because I became a banshee, and all souls can walk freely on Halloween." Lily crossed her arms. "Now I want to know what the hell you were doing the night I was killed. Don't give me all that crap about it being an accident either." One thing she had learnt over the past year was everything happened for a reason. Especially when it came to death. Contrary to what Grim said.

Jared shook his head. "What difference will my telling you make?"

"I deserve an explanation. You owe me at least that much."

"What will it change?"

"It will make up for the questions I've had since you killed me last year."

Jared sighed and leaned back against one of the headstones. "I have been on the run for over a year now."

"Now why doesn't that surprise me?" Lily scoffed. "What did you do? Did you kill someone else?"

"If you want to know maybe you should stop interrupting me."

She sighed and hopped up onto one of the headstones so she could sit down. "Alright, I'm listening."

Jared shook his head. "I still don't see what good telling you will do."

"Confession is good for the soul. You'd be surprised how many people tell me their sins before they move on." She crossed her arms over her chest.

Jared hesitated. "I — I stole something — a magical amulet. I thought it would be the thing I needed to get a load of cash." He shook his head again. "But I'm sick of

49

looking over my shoulder. That thing has brought me nothing but trouble."

Lily forced herself to keep her mouth shut. She had been waiting for an explanation for so long now. She wouldn't lose this opportunity.

"I was running on Halloween last year when I stole the amulet," Jared continued. "I kept opening different portals to lose the person chasing me." He ran a hand through his hair. "The portal I opened on the street that night failed because I was injured and couldn't hold it open long enough to get through. It opened in the wrong place instead of in the house I was hiding in."

"And the bolt of lightning? Where did that come from?" Lily leaned forward. She had replayed those events so many times to figure out what it all meant. It felt a little strange to finally hear the answers.

"It was sent by the person I stole the amulet from. But I am sick of running," Jared said. "I'm sorry for what happened. You were in the wrong place at the wrong time. I know nothing I say or do will make up for that." He raised his arms in surrender. "So, go ahead. Take revenge."

Lily's mouth fell open. "That's it? I died because you stole some magic necklace?" Somehow, she had thought it had been something more insidious than that. It made it sound like her life had meant nothing in the grand scheme of things. Perhaps it hadn't.

"You think I wanted to kill you?" Jared gave a harsh laugh. "I didn't do it out of greed either."

"Okay, so why did you do it?"

A fireball flew towards them.

Outside the graveyard stood the demon who had attacked them back at the Travelodge.

"Is he the one you stole the amulet from?" Lily ducked as another fireball came at them and hit a nearby headstone.

"No."

"Then why is he after you?"

"The person I stole it from must've sent him." Jared put his hands over his head as he dropped to his knees.

"Oh, just give me the amulet and I'll give you a quick death."

"What will you do with it?"

"That's not important." Lily had a good idea what the amulet was — something which Grim desired. If she got it back, she'd get a chance of becoming human again.

"You don't even know what the amulet does. It can grant someone immortality."

More fireballs came at them. Lily reached out to grab his arm. She would take him somewhere, grab the amulet, and kill him.

She would have her revenge and get the chance to live again.

Grim wanted the amulet more than anything.

Instead, Jared grabbed her hand and energy jolted between them.

Images flashed through her mind of what he had been through over the past year.

Lily pulled away. Horrified to realise she felt sorry for him.

He hadn't meant to kill her that night.

Did she feel sorry for the man who killed her?

She had wanted nothing more than to get her revenge on him for an entire year. He was a thief — he would have had a death sentence on his head the moment he stole the amulet. How could she feel sorry for him?

"What are you doing?" she demanded. "If you expect me to spare you —"

"I need your help. I will give you the amulet if you help me escape," Jared said.

Lily sighed. "What makes you think I'll help you?"

"Because I know there is still good in you. I know you are angry about losing your life, but don't you see, you're not a killer," Jared said. "If you were, you would have let that demon finish me off. A witch's duty is to help others."

"Fine, I'll help you," she ground out. "Tell me where the amulet is."

Once she got the amulet, she wouldn't pass up the chance to kill him and get her revenge once and for all.

CHAPTER 4

Lily and Jared reappeared in another disused graveyard on the other side of town. Jared had insisted they needed to go there.

All of the headstones here were weathered or overgrown by brambles. Lily guessed this was where he had hidden the amulet. He hadn't answered when she had asked him about it.

"It's been a year since I last came here. Everything looks even more overground." Jared glanced around, uneasy. "I just hope we weren't followed."

"There are no demons nearby — I would sense then." She found him. "If this amulet grants immortality why didn't you use it? Why hide it?"

Jared shook his head. "Because I never figured out how it works, and I decided the price for immortality was too much. Stealing the amulet had already caused your death. How much more blood would I have on my hands if I kept it and claimed immortality for myself?"

A killer with a conscience. It made her hesitate. Would she be able to kill him?

"What are we looking for?" Lily glanced around at the mass of graves and wondered if he would remember where he had hidden the amulet.

"For a headstone with a fleur-de-lis on it. How are you alive again?" Jared went over to one headstone and then over to another one. "You look and feel so real."

"I'm allowed to regain human form tonight. The dead can walk freely today."

"So, you've been stuck since... Since last year?"

Lily shook her head. "No, I told you. I'm a banshee."

"That doesn't sound good. I thought your soul might be stuck here after... What happened. Being a banshee seems worse somehow. Guess that explains how you screamed so loud at that demon."

Lily waved her hand in dismissal. "It's better than being stuck here, believe me."

During the rare moments when she got time off from her banshee duties, she had tried to convince a few earthbound souls to move on. Sometimes it worked. Most of the time people remained stuck here on earth.

"You could have moved on and found peace," Jared remarked.

"I didn't know how to move on when I lost my life for no reason." Lily checked the next set of headstones but saw no sign of a fleur-de-lis on them. "Plus, being a banshee isn't so bad. Apart from the not-being-able-to-live-my-life-any-more part. The other side doesn't look like all it's cracked up to be."

"Sorry. If I had known what would happen that night, I would never have opened that portal."

"Why did you steal the amulet?" She arched her brow. "How did you even know it existed?"

She couldn't imagine anyone would want to advertise about having an amulet that granted eternal life. Wouldn't someone have kept that to themselves? Lily didn't know much about the amulet or where it came from. Grim had never mentioned it before now. Although she had heard stories from spirits on the other side. The dead liked to gossip as much as the living did.

"I read about it and tracked it down using some old books. It was easier to find than I expected."

"And you haven't used the amulet before?" Lily asked. "I find that hard to believe after the trouble you went to steal it."

"Using the amulet comes with a price — one that I wasn't willing to pay. Besides, it didn't work for me. Since then, I've been stuck with bloody demons trying to kill me all the time.

"Who did you steal it from?" Lily asked, more out of curiosity than because she wanted to help him. Helping him now wouldn't change anything. She was only doing this to find the amulet.

Maybe his death would bring her peace and maybe she could come to terms with the loss of her old life.

"I never knew who the original owner was. I found it hidden in another tomb. That's where I got the idea of hiding it again on holy ground." Jared sighed. "It must be around here somewhere."

Lily placed her hand on one of the stones and images flashed through her eyes. Until she caught sight of Jared holding the amulet in his hand as he stalked by the different headstones.

"Over here." Lily pulled aside some dead brambles until a fleur-de-lis became visible.

Jared rushed over. "This is it. Once we have the amulet, I want you to take it. Do whatever you like with it. I just want it gone." He reached out then hesitated. "Will you let me go after this?"

Lily froze. What could she say? "No way, I'll kill you no matter what."

That would make him run off in fear.

"Let's find the amulet," she said instead.

"Give me a hand."

Together they pushed the stone lid which groaned as it slid out. A blast of light sent them crashing to the ground.

Lily pulled out one of her knives. "It's about time."

Grim stood a few feet away.

"What are you doing here?" Lily demanded.

"I'm here to reclaim what's mine. I needed your help to find it. That's why I killed you last year."

Lily's mouth fell open. "What? That was you? But... I don't understand."

"You were convenient, Lily. I foresaw you would be the one to help me retrieve my amulet." Grim grinned and threw an energy ball at Jared. "That's why I killed you in the first place. I knew you would be so hellbent on revenge that you would stop at nothing to find the person who killed you. You were so easy to manipulate." He chuckled.

Jared screamed as his body exploded. "Why... Why would you do that?" Lily gasped.

"Because he stole from me. I knew you'd be so blinded by revenge you'd lead me straight to my amulet." Grim reached inside the tomb.

Lily let out a bloodcurdling banshee scream and knocked Grim off his feet. She leapt up and yanked the glowing green amulet out and slipped it around her neck.

Grim screamed. "No, that's the source of my power!"

She threw an energy ball at him.

She knew the price that came with the amulet. Now, she was no longer a banshee.

Now, she was the new Grim Reaper and she had finally got her revenge at last.

THE END

Puck's Fate

CHAPTER 1

Eveleigh Alvin jolted awake as the sound of something crashing drew her from sleep. No light came through the curtains, so she knew it must be the middle of the night. She hadn't heard the clock chime though, so she had no idea what time it was.

Raised voices echoed down the hall. Evie rubbed the sleep from her eyes and pushed her long silver hair off her face. She had no idea who her father would be arguing with. Aside from the housekeeper who came in every day, or the cook that lived close by, she and her father lived alone.

Evie climbed out of bed and padded across the floor to the door. She didn't turn the light on as she didn't want her father to know she was awake. The door creaked as she opened it and the arguing grew louder. She cast her senses out and felt her father's familiar presence. Someone else was with him, but the presence remained hidden from her. Outside, the long hallway remained shrouded in darkness. The rich red carpet looked almost black and the red gold walls were just as dark.

Evie hesitated. Should she just go and see if everything was okay? Or should she wait until whoever was in there had left? She padded down the hallway, using only the faint slivers of moonlight shining through the window to see by.

It wasn't odd she couldn't sense the person. A lot of fae often cloaked their presences. It wasn't unusual for her father to have late-night visitors, as he was one of the king's advisers. She guessed someone from the council must have come to see him. But why were they arguing? Evie's heart pounded in her ears as she decided what to do. Maybe she should go in. If her father got angry with her, she'd apologise and ask them to keep the noise down.

Evie made her way down the hall but still couldn't make out what her father and his guest were arguing about. When she reached the top of the staircase, she hesitated again.

"The Eldry girl must die," the other voice snapped. "You were supposed to arrange it."

"You already risked everything when you had Freya Goodwin killed. You can't keep killing people or you will raise too many suspicions," her father said.

Evie froze. No, that was impossible. Her father couldn't be plotting to kill anyone. That didn't sound like him at all. Just because he worked for the Unseelie king, didn't mean he was a bad man. Not all the Unseelie court were bad unlike what most of the Fae believed.

Who was down there and who was the Eldry girl they had mentioned?

The only name that did sound familiar was the name Goodwin. Evie knew Freya Goodwin. She was the heir of the spring court before it had been disbanded, and now only two fae monarchs ruled instead of four.

Had Freya been killed?

Evie believed her father would have mentioned it if she had. He always shared important news with her about the different courts. Unless they meant another Goodwin family member. She knew Freya had sisters but didn't know much about them.

Evie needed to hear more, so she dropped to her knees and crawled along the landing and stopped when she got to the edge of the banister above the sitting room. She stayed down and out of sight for fear her father or whoever was with him might see her.

"The Eldry girl must be gotten rid of," the male voice said.

Evie couldn't make out the man's face in the semidarkness. But she recognised his deep baritone voice. It sounded like the king himself. It was unusual for Gerard to visit her father in person.

"But she's a child — the same age as my daughter. She can't even use her powers," her father said. "Why must she be killed?"

"Because she is a threat to everything the fae stand for," the other man snapped. "We can't have a faeling at the academy, much less one as powerful as her. You know all half breeds go bad. I won't have her putting people at risk."

"You killing Freya was bad enough," her father protested. "I won't take part in hurting a child."

Evie's blood went cold. Freya had been killed. Good goddess, had her father been part of it?

Evie couldn't believe it. Freya had always been kind to her and even sent her books. Why would anyone have her killed?

"You must help me get rid of her. We have no idea who the Eldry girl is or where she came from," the man snapped. "Do you want her destroying what remains of the Ever Realm with her unnatural abilities?"

"We don't know she will do that," her father snapped. "My vision was unclear."

"You said she would destroy the fae courts. That makes her an even bigger threat to the fae than the humans were when they polluted the planet and destroyed half our realm. Do you want all of the fae destroyed?"

Evie wrapped her arms around her knees, unsure what

to do. Whoever Silvana Eldry was, she had to be warned. She had to talk to her father and convince him to do just that.

If only the other man would leave.

"I will play no part in this," her father insisted. "I never thought Freya should have been killed either. She wasn't a threat."

"Freya stole from me and dared to stand against us. She knew about the girl and even became her custodian."

Evie wondered if she should get up and make her presence known. No, that might get her into trouble with that murderous sounding stranger.

Maybe she could glamour herself to look like the housekeeper and pretend to stumble in. Millie, their housekeeper, sometimes came in at night to check the house remained in order.

Think, she told herself. She had to do something to help her father get out of this.

Fear gnawed at her stomach.

"Then you're of no use to me," the man said.

Her father gasped, choking as he struggled for breath. Evie threw caution to the wind and leapt up. Her father collapsed to the floor and a small sound escaped her. She clamped a hand over her mouth, but it was too late. The man had caught sight of her.

King Gerard glared up at her.

Evie knew she had to run. The man threw a fireball at her.

She ducked, and the fireball struck the wall behind her. It ignited the tapestry that hung there.

Evie ran to her room and locked the door behind her. She knew that wouldn't do much good. Instead, she flung open the window. There was no time to grab anything. She had to leave now, or she would meet the same fate as her father.

Evie shoved her feet into some shoes and pulled on a coat. She didn't have time to grab anything else. She scrambled onto the windowsill and wished she had wings to fly. As a Puck, she didn't have the ability to do that. Air rushed past her as she jumped.

Air whooshed from her lungs as she landed in a heap. Evie knew she couldn't stick around, or the killer would find her. Tears stung her eyes, but her father wouldn't have wanted her to give up.

She spared one last look back at her house. The King glared down at her. "You will never speak about what happened tonight to anyone." He raised his hand and hit her with a blast of blue energy.

Evie coughed as the light spread over her body. She ran and headed straight for the woods. Hopefully, the killer would lose sight of her in there. Branches caught at her clothing as she ran. She had no idea where to even run to. Her father had always warned her to stay out of the woods since they were close to the border between the fae Ever Realm and the human world.

Evie stumbled as her foot caught in a branch. Energy jolted through her, her eyes snapped shut and her vision blurred.

Large, wolf-like creatures stalked away from her now-burning house. They were coming straight for her.

The image changed as she saw herself and the creatures as they closed in on her.

Blood roared in her ears. Evie gasped as the vision faded. Good goddess. She had a vision. But that didn't make sense. She was a Puck. Most of the fae considered them tricksters, but the gift of foresight had been passed down through her bloodline for centuries.

Evie had been taught about the visions but hadn't possessed the sight until now. It had always been assumed she didn't possess the gift since she had never been able to get a vision. Her father had spent years testing and training her. Evie had never thought she would get the gift of sight either. Why did it have to be now?

She had thought if she ever got it, she would at least

have her father to help her deal with it. He was gone now. Part of her wanted to curl up in a ball and cry over her loss. Her father was the only family she had. He had never let her attend the Academy like all the other fae her age did.

Evie ran faster. More branches snagged her arms and face. She couldn't let herself be captured. But where would she even run to? She doubted she would find help among her father's friends at the Unseelie court. Not if her father's killer was involved with them.

Where could she go? She had never been to the human world and often didn't understand their ways.

Evie stumbled as she ran headlong into some thorns. The feel of the wolf creature's presence grew stronger.

Evie dodged the thorns and ran faster. Blood pounded in her ears. She wouldn't let that thing catch up with her.

Somehow, she had to find someone who could not only help her but warn Silvana Eldry before anyone had the chance to hurt her.

Light glimmered up ahead, and Evie froze. This was the edge of the Everlight — a border between the human world and what remained of the fae realm. If she went through, she wouldn't be able to return here unless she had help. Her father had always warned her to stay away from the human realm. Humans might not have magic, but they had destroyed half of the fae realm in their desire to control everything.

Evie hesitated, took a deep breath, and stepped into the unknown.

CHAPTER 2

Bright sunlight blinded Evie. She woke up and found herself lying in the dirt. Face first. She groaned, and it took a few moments to realise why she wasn't in bed. Her father was gone. Killed by the same man who'd sent that wolf creature after her. Bits of leaves were stuck in her hair, and one of her pointed ears was caked in dirt.

The night's events all came flooding back like a bad dream, and she remembered how she had crossed over out of the Ever Realm and into the human one.

She groaned and scrambled up into a sitting position. Evie shivered and rubbed the dirt off her face. A fine layer of dew had covered her entire body. Trees surrounded her on all sides, and she found herself in another forest. The trees looked less green here. Darker and more earthy compared to the shimmering trees on the other side of the veil.

Evie wiped the rest of the dirt off her face and scrambled up. Pale slivers of sunlight broke through the murky grey sky. Where was she? And how would she find anyone to help her?

She wrapped her arms around herself. A few tears streaked down her dirty face.

Her father was gone, and she would be dead too if she didn't find somewhere safe to hide.

"Don't give up, Eveleigh," her father's voice came to her.

Evie spun around but found no sign of her father anywhere. Where had his voice come from? Had his spirit been there with her? Or had it just been a figment of her imagination?

She would have given anything to see her father again. To have the chance to say goodbye to him and tell him how much she loved him. She opened her mouth to call out for him, then closed it. Those wolf creatures could be somewhere nearby, and she didn't want to risk leading them straight to her. Her stomach grumbled with hunger and her throat felt dry.

Evie pushed her way through the trees but knew she needed to figure out her next move. She pressed her palm against a tree trunk and waited for a vision to come to her.

Nothing happened.

She gritted her teeth. The human realm had a strange energy around it, unlike the natural warmth and brightness of the Ever Realm. She had to find food and shelter, then figure out her next move. How she wished her father had brought her to this world more.

Hadn't he known something might happen to him? Had he not foreseen it?

Evie found it hard to believe her father hadn't had some inkling about what would happen. He had always been good at controlling his abilities.

She pushed her way through the trees and spotted some berries. Her stomach grumbled at the sight, but she hesitated. What if they were poisonous? She didn't want to risk dying before she had a chance to tell someone what she knew. She would make sure her father's death wasn't in vain.

Evie picked up a few berries and waited. No vision came to her. On closer inspection, she realised they weren't poisonous. She couldn't remember the name of them, but she had seen the cook using them before. She gulped down a few, then froze when the sound of voices drifted her way.

Two young women, no, girls, who looked to be about the same age as her, were headed in her direction.

"Remind me again why we are out here." The first one had long silvery blond hair and blue eyes.

The other girl was taller, more athletic, with blue eyes and long curly brown hair. She waved her hand in exasperation. "I thought it would do you good to get out of the castle for a while. It's okay to talk about it."

The blonde girl shook her head. "There's nothing to talk about. She's gone. What else is there to say?"

Neither of the girls appeared to have wings. It made Evie wonder if they were humans or not. If they were, they probably wouldn't be any help to her. She needed help from the fellow fae.

"I still think you need to talk about it. Your wings still haven't come back out," the brunette said. "That's a sign of —"

"I am not repressing anything. Holy crackers, I swear I'll scream if you say that again."

Evie winced. The blonde girl had so much repressed emotion inside her. It felt like a dam waiting to break. Evie had always been good at sensing emotions, even if she hadn't had visions.

"Right, keep telling yourself that," the brunette said.

"Mel, I'm not in the mood for chitchat." The blonde girl pushed her way through the trees.

Evie retreated further back. She didn't want to risk being seen. As much as she wanted to find help, she knew she couldn't trust anyone so easily. She had to watch these two first and figure out what they were. Only then could she decide if they would help or not.

"Freya's legacy reading is in a few days. I thought you could use a break after the memorial," Mel said.

"Mel, we are supposed to be gathering herbs for class. Let's focus on that." The blonde girl stalked off.

Mel froze and Evie turned and ran. She didn't want to be seen. She needed to hide or…

Branches snagged at her clothing as she ran. Why had she stuck around? Those girls wouldn't be able to help her. She needed to get to the Goodwin estate. Freya's family might be the only ones who would believe her story. Evie doubted they were involved in her death. Yet she knew she had no way to get there. She had never been there before, and she'd need to find a transportation ring to travel to their estate. Fae estates were usually shielded, and people could only get there by invitation or if they knew the way.

Evie stumbled. In the distance loomed a castle, and she gasped.

Everlight Academy. She would know the place anywhere. She had dreamt of attending it for half her life, but her father always refused to let her go there. She never understood why.

Evie paused. As a teacher, Freya had lived there for most of the year. Maybe someone here could help her. But who could she trust?

A part of Evie wanted to run to the Academy. Another part of her wanted to run away and hide somewhere else.

Someone blurred in front of her before Evie could even blink.

Mel.

"What the hell do you think you are doing by spying on me and my friend?" Mel demanded.

Evie stared at the girl, mouth agape. How had Mel moved so fast? No fae could move with so much supernatural speed. What was Mel? She had moved like that wolf creature that she had seen last night.

Had Mel come to kill her?

Evie grabbed a stick from the forest floor to defend herself and opened her mouth to speak, but no words would come out. She tried again but still, no sound escaped.

"Whoa!" Mel raised her hands. "I'm not going to attack you. I came to find out why you're spying on us."

Evie hesitated, unsure what to do. Why couldn't she say anything? Her heart pounded in her ears. She thought back to last night when her father's killer had cast a spell on her. He had said something about her not being able to tell anyone what had happened. Had he cursed her somehow?

Mel had an odd energy about her. Like lightning. Fast and strong. Unlike any other fae, Evie had met before.

"Are you alright?" Mel persisted. "Are you hurt? Judging by your looks, I'm guessing you're not from the Academy since you don't look like anyone from here. What happened? Why are you here in the middle of the woods?"

Evie opened her mouth and only a croaking sound came out. Something stung around her throat. She knew then she had been cursed. Her father's killer had made sure she wouldn't talk, so she couldn't expose him. Good goddess, what would she do now? How could she get help if she couldn't speak to anyone? She turned and ran back into the woods.

She needed to hide and figure out her next move.

Mel blurred in front of her again. "Hey, it's okay. No one is going to hurt you."

Tears stung Evie's eyes. Exhaustion and grief weighed heavy on her.

Why couldn't Mel just leave her alone?

"Do you need help?" Mel added. Evie hesitated. "And guessing by the look of you, you do. You look like you've been out here all night. Come on, I'll take you back to the Academy and —"

Evie tried to scream but still, no sound came out. She couldn't go to the Academy. Someone there might take her before the council, and then she would be exposed to her father's killer.

Evie shook her head. She didn't know how else to communicate with Mel.

"Hey, you're bleeding. What happened?" Mel grabbed Evie's arm where she had caught it on some brambles.

A vision slammed into Evie before she had the chance to say anything.

The wolf creature was here. It had come for her again.

CHAPTER 3

Evie gasped as the vision faded. "What the hell was that?" Mel asked and still held onto Eve's wrist.

A growling sound chilled Evie's blood and all colour drained from her face.

Oh goddess, she was going to die.

It has found me.

The wolf creature emerged from behind the trees.

"Oh, goody." Mel shoved Evie behind her. "I've been dying to get my hands on one of these again."

Again? Mel had faced this creature before?

Evie couldn't fathom how that was possible.

Don't. It will kill you! Evie thought. *We need to run.* But of course, Mel didn't hear her. Evie didn't know how to communicate with people in thought.

"Don't worry. I'm a Guardian. I can handle a lycan."

A Fey Guardian. The enforcers who had once protected the humans and kept miscreant fae in line. She had thought there were none left, but she had heard rumours one worked at the Academy. Fey guardians were warriors blessed with supernatural strength and speed. Even so, Evie didn't want Mel to die because the lycan had come for her.

No, please don't. Evie placed a hand on her shoulder. *I don't want you to get hurt. It's here for me.* She shook her head again.

The lycan lunged towards them, but Mel ignored her.

Evie raised her stick again. It wasn't much of a weapon, but it was definitely better than nothing. She wasn't about to roll over and die.

Mel raised her hand and a glowing wall of energy flashed in front of them. It blocked the lycan's advances. Mel then pulled out a knife and drew strange symbols in the air with it. The lycan continued to thrash against the ward. Light swirled around the lycan as a portal swept it away.

Evie breathed a sigh of relief.

"Don't worry, it's gone. For now. I only sent it into the fae realm. I need a lot more energy to send it into the underworld." Mel put her hands on her hips. "You're coming back to the Academy with me. And you better start explaining why that thing was after you."

Evie shook her head and motioned to her throat. Then shook her head again.

Mel frowned. "Are you saying you can't speak?"

Evie nodded and lowered her eyes.

Mel blew out a breath. "That's going to make things much harder. Don't worry, we'll figure something out.

Evie sniffed. How would she ever be able to tell anyone about her father's murder and what had happened to him? How would she get any help?

"Like I said, I'm a Guardian. I'm not going to let anyone hurt you. You can trust me."

I don't even know you. Evie wiped her eyes with the back of her sleeve.

"I can find somewhere safe for you to stay in the Academy."

Evie hesitated. She sensed Mel was being sincere and truthful.

Besides, what other choice did she have? She couldn't

keep running forever. She had nowhere else to run to. Maybe the Academy would be the safest place for her.

Evie stifled a scream when Mel used her speed to carry her back inside the castle. But Mel moved so fast no one would have been able to see Evie.

Mel didn't stop moving until they appeared in a small bedroom. It appeared unlived in and there was only a mattress bed, wardrobe, chest of drawers, and an empty bookcase.

Mel let go of Evie and set her back on her feet.

What was this place? Evie frowned.

Mel must have noticed her confusion. "Technically, this is my room, or at least it was. I stayed here when I first got to the Academy, but I moved to a different room when I heard my roommate was joining," Mel explained. "But no one else wants to stay here because they're afraid of me being a Guardian. You can stay here without fear of being seen." Mel motioned to another door. "There's a bathroom through there. You can shower and freshen up whilst I get you some clothes and food."

Evie turned, then hesitated. Why was Mel helping her? Mel didn't know her. She glanced around the room. It looked so bare and unthreatening. This was almost too good to be true. She couldn't understand why anyone, much less a Guardian, would help her. It made no sense.

Guardians were a thing of nightmares to the fae. They didn't help people — not the fae, at least from what she'd heard.

Was Mel in league with the man who had killed her father? Evie couldn't be sure of anything anymore.

"I know what it's like to be on the run and in fear of your life," Mel replied. "Not too long ago, I went through the same thing. I will be back soon." Mel blurred out of the room before Evie could say another word.

Evie headed into the white-tiled bathroom and locked the door behind her. She discarded her dirty clothes and sighed when the hot water from the shower washed over her. It felt like pure bliss after the cold night she had spent in the woods. She wondered what would happen next.

Evie spent the next few days hiding out in the abandoned room. She tried to tell Mel what happened, but so far, they still hadn't found a way to communicate with each other.

Mel came in that morning with more food. "Hey, did you sleep okay?"

Evie wrapped a blanket around herself.

"Sorry, it's not much." Mel placed a couple of pieces of toast, a jar of jam, and two bottles of water on the bed. "I can't take too much without raising suspicion." She chuckled. "I think my friends think I have gone insane."

Evie picked up the toast and took a bite. The toast had already grown cold, but she didn't care. She was too hungry to mind.

"Hey, don't you think it's time to tell me what happened to you?"

Evie hesitated. She wished she could tell Mel what happened. But how could she when her father's killer had cursed her to never speak again?

"I know someone is after you. Or else they wouldn't have sent that lycan," Mel continued.

Evie carried on eating.

"You could at least tell me your name."

Evie opened her mouth, but no words came out. She shook her head.

"What are you afraid of?"

"Everything," Evie wanted to say. "But I can't speak or else I would tell you."

Evie had been trying to figure out a way of communicating with Mel, but so far nothing had worked. She had even tried writing things down, but the words disappeared as soon as she wrote them. The killer's curse made sure she couldn't tell anyone what happened.

"There must be some way we can talk to each other."

73

Mel sighed and started making strange gestures with her hands. "Can you speak sign language? I watched a few videos online." She made more strange gestures. "Do you understand that?"

Evie patted her throat, then shook her head.

Mel frowned. "Okay, no sign language. The videos I watched were about human sign language. Do the fae have their own kind of sign language?"

Evie shrugged and had no idea what Mel was talking about.

"You could write it down here." Mel pulled out a rectangular looking device, tapped on it, and held it out to Evie.

Evie frowned. Mel had told her it was a mobile phone, but people could write on it as well. They had tried using it to communicate with each other more than once. But despite trying everything, whether it be writing on screen or writing on paper, nothing worked.

"Just type the letters and write out whatever you want to say," Mel encouraged.

Evie shook her head again. It wouldn't do any good. The words would only disappear again.

Mel sighed and tapped the screen. She handed the phone to Eve.

On the screen it said: what's your name?

Evie pressed the letters to her name and waited. The words didn't disappear. She gasped and handed the phone to Mel.

"Evie?" Mel grinned. "Is that your name?"

Evie nodded and beamed. Finally, Mel had understood her.

Evie grabbed the phone and typed out: I was cursed so I can no longer speak. The words then faded. Her heart sank. Why had it let her tell Mel her name, but wouldn't let her tell anything else?

She slumped back against the wall and bit back a sob.

"What's wrong?" Mel asked. "You wrote your name.

74

Why can't you write more?"

Evie put her head in her hands. This was hopeless.

She gasped as her eyes snapped shut. A shadow burst through the window and came straight towards her.

She grabbed Mel's hand as the vision faded. "What's wrong?" Mel asked in alarm.

Evie tugged on her arm and dragged her towards the door. They had to get out of there before the thing came after them.

"Wait, Evie, what's wrong?"

Glass shattered as the shadow burst in.

"Oh crap," Mel exclaimed and raised her hand. A glowing ward of energy flared to life.

The wraith burst straight through it.

"Okay, now would be a good time to run." Mel grabbed hold of Evie and blurred them both out of the room.

They reappeared in another, much larger room and stayed there for a few moments. It was a while before they headed back to Evie's room. Mel did her best to use magic to fix the window. She then set more wards in place that would hopefully protect Evie. She told Evie the wraith was unlikely to come back.

Evie didn't want to stay in that room any longer, but knew she didn't have much of a choice.

Mel finished the runes on the windowsill of the room. She bit her lip and came to stand in front of Evie.

"Evie, you need to tell me who is after you," Mel looked desperate to find answers now.

The bedroom door burst open and the blonde girl Evie had seen in the forest a few days earlier came in. "Mel, what's going on?" The girl placed her hands on her hips and Evie knew her secret had been blown.

CHAPTER 4

Evie sagged against the wall. The weight of repressed grief coming from the other girl threatened to overwhelm her. She winced.

"Silvy, what the hell are you doing here?" Mel said and frowned.

"I came to find out what you're hiding." Silvy eyed Evie. "Who is she? What is that around her neck?"

"This is Evie. I found her in the woods a few days ago," Mel explained. "There's nothing on her throat. She is in trouble, but she can't talk." Evie put her head in her hands again. No one could understand her. It was only a matter of time before her father's killer caught up with her.

"I'm not surprised by that spell around her neck."

"There's a spell on her?" Mel's eyes widened.

"Yeah, can't you see it?"

Evie blinked. The girl could see the curse? This was her chance. She mouthed out the words *help me*, desperate for her help.

"I don't see anything," Mel added.

She came over and placed a finger on her throat. Evie grabbed the girl's hands. Evie hesitated. The girl must be an aura reader — a rare gift among the fae. She might be the one person who can understand Evie.

Evie gasped as light exploded around her.

Silvy smiled and nodded. "Now that's better."

Mel winced. "Evie, are you okay?"

"I...I can talk," Evie rasped. A beaming smile broke out on her face. "Thank you, Silvy. You have no idea what you've done for me."

Mel narrowed her eyes. "Silvy, how did you do that?"

Silvy shrugged. "I saw it in her aura. Evie, I can tell you're terrified of someone. What happened to you?"

"My father — they killed my father. He – he refused to kill you, Silvana Eldry." The relief of finally being able to say those words hit her like a ton of bricks.

"Wow, this is huge. We need to go and find Zoe," Mel gasped.

"Wait, are you saying your father killed Freya?" Evie could hear the chill in Silvy's voice.

"No... I don't know." Confusion swirled in her mind. Her father had never directly admitted he was the one who had killed Freya. Was it the king, then? "The person who killed my father did it. I couldn't see them."

"Zoe might be able to help us figure out what happened," Mel said. "Let's go find her and tell her everything we know."

Silvy looked at her and nodded. She vaguely heard Silvy say something to Mel before Silvy stalked off. Mel glanced at her and smiled gently. "Don't worry, Evie. We'll do everything we can to help you."

The end

Fae Born

CHAPTER 1

Freya Goodwin winced as the rusted door creaked open. *I'm never drinking alcohol again after this.* Her head throbbed, and she'd done nothing but feel sick from drinking too much wine a couple of days ago. Yet her friends all looked fine.

"You'll wake the dead with all that racket," her boyfriend, Lucas Melrose, grumbled at their friend, Gerard.

Freya kept her mouth shut and took Lucas's hand. She didn't want to annoy Gerard. He had a nasty temper. She had only agreed to come along on this little expedition because their friend, Maeve, had convinced her to.

As fae royals, all four of them had grown up together. Freya wouldn't say they were friends with Gerard, though.

They all had recently graduated but decided to spend part of the summer holidays at the academy doing extra study, but really it was just for the chance to get away from their parents and have free rein over the castle and enjoy things before they went home.

Gerard was determined to explore a part of the castle that had been sealed off for centuries. Freya would have preferred to just to lie down. Maeve and Gerard loved to drink, whereas she and Lucas preferred to either spend time in the library together or be outside.

"What do you even expect to find?" Freya shivered as she trailed after Gerard and Maeve.

"There could be any number of treasures down here." Gerard grinned. He moved a glowing orb further in to reveal a long narrow passageway beyond the door.

"This part of the castle must have been locked up for good reason," Lucas remarked.

Maeve snorted. "You are such a wimp. Honestly, you two need to learn to have a sense of adventure."

"We are usually the ones who get into trouble when you two mess about," Freya retorted and pushed her long blond hair off her face.

"Stop being such a stick in the mud, Goodwin. Let's explore." Gerard stalked down the passage.

"You can leave if you want to." Maeve flicked her mane of long red hair over her shoulder and hurried after Gerard. "We don't need you to explore the sealed off chamber."

"Maybe we should go," Lucas mused. "Let them have their adventure."

Freya sighed. "No, there might be unknown dangers in here. We should stick together. At least until they have looked around."

"Let them look after themselves. It's not your job to take care of them," Lucas protested.

"They're both heirs, too. If our parents manage to claim their courts back, we'll need to learn to work together." She gave him a quick kiss. "Thanks for being so supportive."

Lucas groaned. "I'm only doing it for you. I still say we should have found somewhere else to stay over the summer holidays."

They trailed after their friends. The passageway widened to reveal several closed doors.

"What a waste of space," Gerard muttered.

The passageway soon ended in another sealed off door. This one looked even older and more rusted than the previous one they had opened.

Freya winced as Gerard wrenched a crowbar against it.

"Did you bring any oil with you? That would probably make it easier to open." Lucas crossed his arms. With his scruffy dark hair and bookish appearance, he looked very different from the muscular Gerard.

Gerard had a mop of dark hair and piercing, cold blue eyes. Beside him, Maeve stood looking like the true princess she was—with her long red hair, dark eyes and glossy designer black dress.

"Of course not. I'm not getting my hands dirty," Gerard grumbled. "Why won't it open?"

"Probably because it's been sealed off for the last five hundred years." Freya pushed her hair off her face and sipped water from her bottle. Her stomach recoiled, and she had to force herself to swallow.

"Are you still feeling sick?" Lucas put a hand to her forehead. "You don't feel warm."

"I'll be alright."

She couldn't understand why Maeve and Gerard were so eager to explore this part of the academy. This place had been sealed up and probably had nothing inside it except spiders and centuries of dust.

"I told you we should just use magic," Maeve snapped. "Blast it open. There are no wards or protection spells on the door, is there?"

Gerard shook his head. "I checked the door and didn't find anything."

"Maybe you should just leave it. We don't know what condition this part of the castle is in." Freya didn't know why the door gave her such a bad feeling. Maybe it was just because of her constant nausea.

"We are going to get through." Gerard put the crowbar down and instead hit it with the full weight of his body.

The door still refused to budge.

"Stand back." Maeve flicked her hair over her shoulder. "I'll get through." She raised her hand and a fireball formed between her fingers. Her magic exploded against the door and left scorch marks, but otherwise the door appeared unharmed. Maeve sighed. "Freya, you have air magic. See if you can open it."

Freya winced. She didn't want to open the door. What if something bad had been locked away in there? This part of the castle hadn't been maintained, so it could be uninhabitable. They could be putting their lives at risk.

She hesitated.

"Come on, Goodwin. Or are you afraid the spiders will get you?" Gerard mocked.

Freya winced. "No, I'm not." She hit the door with a current of air.

Maybe if she opened the damn thing, she and Lucas could make their excuses and leave. The door vibrated against the onslaught of her magic. Gerard threw his weight against it again and it finally creaked open.

Freya kept hold of Lucas's hand as they headed into the first room. "Do you see anything?" she whispered to him.

As an aura reader, Lucas could see things others couldn't.

Lucas furrowed his brow. "No, nothing. It's so dark in here."

They all summoned orbs of glowing light which chased away the shadows. The room appeared to be empty. Nothing but bare grey stone walls and a dirty flagstone floor.

Freya bit her lip. "We should never have told them about that book that mentioned artefacts being hidden away in the castle."

She and Lucas had been drunk at the time. Gerard had made fun of them for being boring. So they had told him of their recent find in the library. A book that contained legends about the academy. Including a secret chamber.

"They are only legends," Lucas muttered. "There won't

be anything to find."

They checked the next two rooms, which were empty.

They found Maeve and Gerard in a much larger room. It seemed empty too, apart from a large hole in the floor.

"Looks like a well shaft," Lucas observed. "See, I told you there would be nothing to find here."

"That's not true. Look." Gerard motioned to the well. "There's something glowing down there."

Freya peered into the gloom. Something shimmered at the bottom of the narrow shaft.

Gerard sent his orb down into the well, but they couldn't make anything out. "Someone needs to fly down there," Gerard insisted.

"How? It's too narrow." Lucas shook his head. "None of us would fit."

Maeve scowled. "I'm not going down there. Freya should go. She is the thinnest."

Freya clutched her still-churning stomach. "I'm not going." She raised her hands and sent a current of air down the well, but the glowing object wouldn't budge.

"You're the smallest, Goodwin. Go down and see what it is," Gerard snapped.

"Lay off her, would you?" Lucas glowered at him. "She said no."

"How else are we going to find those artefacts you told us about?" Maeve pouted. "You made the story sounds so exciting. Finding buried treasure here at the academy would be thrilling."

"Let's go, Lucas," Freya said. "I'm not—" Gerard cut her off and shoved her into the well.

Freya screamed as she fell. Her hands reached out to grab onto something to slow her descent. She didn't have time to get her wings out either. She hit the bottom of the well and winced. Her back and legs ached from her hard landing.

"Have you gone bloody mad?" Lucas shouted at Gerard.

Good goddess, she had never thought Gerard would push her in. Why hadn't she left when she had the chance? If Maeve and Gerard wanted to find buried treasure, then they could do it by themselves. She wanted no part in this. She just wanted to be alone with her boyfriend for a while. And to lie down until this awful sickness passed.

"Freya, are you alright?" Lucas called down to her. "Are you hurt?" He knelt at the edge of the shaft. "It's too narrow for me to reach you."

"I think so." She scrabbled up. Her lip curled at the mud and debris that now covered her dress.

"Get the glowing object," Gerard called out. "Can you see what it is?"

Freya had half a mind to fly back up and refuse to get whatever it was, but curiosity got the better of her. She reached out and dug through the mud.

"It's a box," she called up to them.

It took a few more attempts, but finally she pulled it free. It was a wooden box, with a glowing light coming from it.

"Great, bring it up." Gerard sounded excited, and Maeve gave a squeal of delight.

Freya wondered what she had got herself into as she unfurled her wings and flew back toward the surface.

CHAPTER 2

"You almost killed Freya for a box?" Lucas glowered at Gerard as he wiped more grime off the box.

Freya brushed herself down, she would need a bath and a good scrub after this.

"A box with something important in it." Gerard grinned. "Nice work, Goodwin. For once you being small works in your favour."

"Open it," Maeve demanded. "I want to know what's inside. Are you sure there wasn't anything else at the bottom of that well, Freya?"

Freya scraped more mud off her arms. "Even if there was, I'm not going back down there to look."

Gerard tugged at the box, but it didn't budge. "It's locked."

"Can we please get out of here?" Freya said. "This place gives me the creeps."

Maeve and Gerard insisted on looking around for a while longer and went through each room again one by one. Gerard refused to put the box down. Too bad. Freya would have liked to get her hands on it and have a glimpse of it for herself. After all, she'd been the one who'd recovered it. Shouldn't she have had the first look?

After a few more failed attempts at opening the box, Gerard and Maeve finally agreed to leave the sealed off area.

Freya headed back to the room she shared with Lucas and showered. It took forever to get all the grime off. She also gulped down an anti-sickness potion, which seemed to settle her stomach. She changed into a clean dress and found Lucas at his desk, reading.

"I can't find anything in here to explain what might be in that box." He sighed. "Goddess, I hope they haven't found anything dangerous. We should never have told them that story."

"Well, I don't plan on drinking with them ever again." Freya put her hands on his shoulders. "We only have a couple more weeks here, then we can move to the human world like we planned."

She knew running away with Lucas would make her family unhappy, but they had been together a couple of years now. Dating in secret. Despite her family's reservations, she loved him with all her heart and couldn't wait to start their new life together.

They had to wait until the summer solstice to cross over into the human realm. The veil between the fae Ever realm and the human realm always grew thinner on that day.

"Good, because I can't take much more of Gerard and Maeve," Lucas grumbled. "At least we're bonded now. Our families could never split us apart."

Freya glanced at the glowing blue vines around her left wrist. A sign she and Lucas now shared a bonded soul, that went far beyond marriage in the fae world. They would be linked to each other forever now.

She smiled and gave him a quick kiss.

Adjusting to the human world would take time, but she knew they could handle anything as long as they stayed together. Plus, her best friend, Clarissa, came from the human world and would be there to help them.

Someone banged on the door and made them both jump.

Freya sighed when she sensed Maeve's presence. "She's probably come to tell us what she's found."

Lucas groaned. "Or to get us to help them figure out what it is. We should dispose of the box and make sure no one opens it."

"But what if there is an important historical artefact in there?" Freya furrowed her brow. "Something like that would be priceless."

"It could get all of us killed." Lucas turned his attention back to his books.

Freya headed over and opened the door. "What's wrong? Did you manage to open the box?"

"Gerard can't open the box, but we cleaned it up a bit. You need to come and help us." Maeve crossed her arms and scowled. "How hard can it be to open one stupid box?"

Lucas raised his hands. "I want no part in this. Your idiot boyfriend already put Freya's life at risk when—"

"Oh, stop being so dramatic, Luc. That box contains the kind of treasure you two bookworms love reading about. Come on, we need you to read the inscription on the box." Maeve headed out before either of them could protest further.

Freya took his hand. "Let's see what it says. You're better at the old fae dialects than I am."

Lucas groaned again but rose to his feet. "Fine, but we're not opening it."

They found Maeve and Gerard around a table in the great library.

Dirt covered the table from where Gerard had scraped it off with a knife. Freya hoped he hadn't done any damage to the box. She wished he would be more careful. The box itself could be fragile, and he could potentially damage anything inside it.

"Finally!" Gerard crossed his arms. "What took you so

long? I thought you two would be more excited about this find."

"We were busy," Lucas snapped. "You can't—"

Freya put her hand on his shoulder to silence him. "Gerard, what do you need help with?"

"What does this thing say?" Gerard glowered at Lucas and motioned toward the box.

They both peered closer. "It's an old fae dialect," Lucas remarked. "It's a warning to not open the box or great evil will befall whoever does."

Gerard scoffed at that. "You're lying. You just don't want us to open it."

Freya peered closer. "He's right. It says the box must remain sealed."

"Then what's inside?" Maeve wanted to know. "Is it something valuable? Like one of those famous artefacts you were telling us about the other night?"

"It doesn't say." Lucas should his head. "That warning is good enough for me. Freya, let's go."

"Come on, Freya," Maeve gave her a hard look. "You want to know what's in there, don't you?"

Freya hesitated. "I'd like to know, too."

Lucas stared at her in disbelief. "Fine. If that's what you want, good luck." He stormed off without saying another word.

Freya flinched and her heart ached. Why couldn't he be more supportive of this?

Maeve rolled her eyes. "Don't know what you see in him. He is such a stick in the mud."

"He's just being cautious." Freya picked up the box to see if it had anything else written on it, but found nothing. "It looks like we need a key."

"The key has probably been lost for centuries. We have no way of finding it," Gerard complained. "We'll just have to unlock it ourselves."

"I'll do it." Maeve raised her hand and fire appeared between her fingers.

"Don't!" Freya held up her hand. "You might destroy whatever is in the box."

"She's right." Gerard swatted Maeve's hand away.

Maeve scowled at him. "How else can we open it? I doubt we'll find the key lying around."

"I already tried a crowbar. None of the tools I found in the maintenance cupboard worked." Gerard glowered at the box. "Maeve, try burning the lock but be careful."

Fire appeared between Maeve's fingers. She singed around the lock, but it still didn't open.

Freya summoned a current of air, but nothing happened.

"Give me a few days to research and I'll—" Freya said.

Gerard didn't look happy to hear that. "Days? You expect us to wait that long?"

Gerard was used to getting whatever he wanted whenever he demanded it. Such was a perk of being a fae prince.

"We can't always have what we want," Freya snapped. "Give me time. I might be able to figure out what's inside before we open it. At least we can make sure it's nothing dangerous that way."

Maeve sighed. "Fine, do your research, but don't open it without us."

She headed back to her room with the box and hoped she could figure it out.

Lucas gasped at her when she walked in with it. "You've got to be joking. Freya—"

She held up a hand to silence him. "Don't. We were lucky to get this away from them." She closed the door behind her. "We need to find out what's inside."

That meant they spent a few days doing research in the library. And fending off endless questions and pestering from Maeve and Gerard. Lucas insisted they dispose of the box, but despite the warning Freya was eager to find out what lay inside.

"We are running out of time," Lucas said at breakfast

that morning. "We need to get rid of it before Maeve and Gerard find a way to open it."

"There must be a way to open the thing." Freya frowned at the box. She twirled her finger as she summoned a current of air.

She felt relieved her nausea had finally worn off, it always felt worse in the morning. She'd been so busy doing research on the box she hadn't had time to figure out what might be causing it.

After a few seconds, the lock clicked open.

Her heart leapt as she pulled the lid open. Inside lay small glowing orb.

"It's a stone. The Everlight stone," Freya gasped.

"We can't be sure of that." Lucas shook his head. "The accounts of it are mixed. No one has ever been sure of its power or what it looks like."

"There's a portrait back in my family home of my ancestor Lana Goodwin. In the portrait she is holding a stone just like this." Freya couldn't keep the excitement out of her voice and rubbed her hands together. "There's always been a legend in my family that we once possessed the stone. This must be it."

"Let's do some thorough research before we do anything with it. We'll keep delaying Maeve and Gerard for as long as we can."

Freya bit her lip. "Maybe we should take the stone with us to the human world. At least that way they wouldn't be able to access it at all."

Lucas shook his head. "But we still have more than a week before the solstice. I doubt we'll be able to delay them that long."

"We'll find a way." She gave him another quick kiss. "One way or another, we will keep the stone safe from them."

CHAPTER 3

Freya spent the next few days doing research on the stone, while still fighting off her lingering nausea. But she didn't have time to worry about it. When she got to the human world, she would figure out what was causing it.

Deciding she needed a break; she ran outside to meet her best friend, Clarissa Greenwood. She had been surprised when Clarissa had called her. She hadn't thought Clarissa could come through the portal again until the solstice.

Freya threw her arms around her friend. "It's so good to see you." She squeezed Clarissa. "How did you get through?"

"I managed to open the portal and get through using the standing stone that's nearby." Clarissa bit her lip and brushed her long blond hair off her face. "I've got another problem and I needed someone to talk to."

"What?" Freya furrowed her brow.

"I'm pregnant."

Freya's mouth fell open. "What? How?"

Clarissa rolled her eyes. "The usual way."

"No, I didn't mean that. I mean, how could you let that happen? There are spells to protect against that." Freya couldn't believe it. How could Clarissa have been so careless? At nineteen, she was too young. Freya couldn't imagine becoming a mother at such a young age.

Clarissa shook her head. "I'm half witch and a Guardian. I didn't think a fae could get me pregnant. Besides, I didn't really think about it at the time since I was wasted."

"You're a Fey Guardian. That means you still have fae magic, at least in part." Freya put her hand on Clarissa's arm. "Are you going to keep it?"

She shrugged. "I don't know. Maybe. But you have to promise not to tell anyone. I don't want the father to know."

"Who is the father?" Freya's frown deepened. She didn't remember Clarissa having a boyfriend, at least not a regular one when they had been here at the academy. For the most part, she hadn't been interested in romance.

Clarissa hesitated. "Promise you won't get angry at me?"

"Why would I be angry?"

"Because he's already involved with someone. Someone you know pretty well."

Her heart lurched. "What do you mean? Who is it?"

Clarissa hadn't dated much when they had been here at the academy. She couldn't imagine who the father might be. Clarissa had to be a few months along since they had graduated three months ago.

Clarissa bit her lip. "It's Gerard." She held up her hand when Freya opened her mouth to speak. "I already know what you're going to say. Yeah, it was a mistake. We were drunk and I wasn't thinking clearly. I already regret what happened, and I know Maeve would go ballistic if she ever found out. Which is why you have to promise you won't tell her anything."

Freya's mouth fell open. "But he and Maeve are talking about getting married." She couldn't believe it. "Good goddess, I knew he was a slimy rat, but I thought he would be faithful to Maeve." She shook her head. "No, I won't tell anyone. I'm not judging you either. But what are you going to do? How are you going to support a child on your own?"

"I'm not telling him. He's a dog and I don't want him to be part of my life." Clarissa's hands clenched into fists. "Or my child's—if I keep it."

"How are you gonna keep something like that a secret?" Freya asked. "Any child you have could have Gerard's powers. You can't hide that."

"It might not even have fae powers." Clarissa shook her head. "Enough talk of this. It's still early. This pregnancy might not even last. You know how rare fae pregnancies are." She sat down on the grass verge. "Let's talk about something else. Are you and Lucas still gonna move to the human world?"

Freya shrugged. "I hope so. But things have been a little strained between us the past few days."

Freya told her about how they had found the stone and how distant Lucas had been since then. She hated being at odds with him, but she couldn't give up on the stone. She needed to know what it was and what it could do.

"Can I see the stone?" Clarissa asked.

Freya took her up to her room. Lucas had gone to the library to do more research, and Maeve and Gerard were probably still in bed.

"Here it is." Freya opened the box and took the stone out. "There is an inscription on it, but I haven't been able to read it yet."

"Oh, I know this language." Clarissa nodded. "It's an old dialect. It says it contains each unique element and can be used to form a bridge between the two realms. It contains the true power of the Everlight."

The Everlight. The very force used by the goddess to create the first fae. The very thing that had given life to their realm and their race.

"This is incredible," Freya breathed. "This stone is

thought to have been lost for centuries. Most people think it's a myth."

"You can't let Maeve and Gerard have it. It's bad enough they will both rule the fae courts one day." Clarissa shuddered. "If this thing is the Everlight stone, we need to get out of here and hide it someplace."

"If they found out, I take it they'd never stop looking for it. I think they know what it is. That's why they were so desperate to find it."

Goddess, how could she have been so blind not to notice before now?

Maeve and Gerard were never interested in anything unless it served some sort of purpose for them. They thrived on power and always had.

"Take this." Freya held the stone out to her. "Go through the portal and take it with you."

"What about you? Maeve and Gerard will freak when they find out. Why don't you come with me? You want to leave anyway. Let's go now. I can get you through." Clarissa smiled. "We don't have to wait until the solstice. One good thing about being pregnant is my powers are a lot stronger."

Freya hesitated. She'd been dreaming of going away for weeks. Now that dream was in her grasp, she didn't feel excited. Instead, she felt anxious. "I can't go without Lucas. We're bonded now. I'll get him and we will leave straightaway."

"Hurry, I'll be waiting for you at the portal." Clarissa turned away.

She had always envied her ability to move at supernatural speed.

Freya gathered up her belongings in a bag and hurried down to the library. To her dismay, she heard Gerard talking in there.

Goddess damn it, she couldn't risk running into him or he'd ask about the stone.

Lucas, I need you. She reached out to him with her mind.

Clarissa is here. She can take us through the portal right now. We need to leave immediately. Get away from Gerard.

Why? What's wrong? Lucas sounded concerned.

I found out the stone is the Everlight stone.

That's impossible! Lucas protested. *It's just a myth.*

No, it's not. Clarissa read the inscription on it. Gerard and Maeve must know what it is. We need to leave. Right now. If they think we're taking it, they will turn on us. Clarissa can get us through the portal.

Get to the portal. I'll be there as fast as I can.

Freya's heart leapt. *Be careful. Act normal or Gerard will suspect you.*

She didn't want to leave without him. But she knew she couldn't delay getting to the portal. They had to be ready to step through.

Freya hurried downstairs and out the back door. She didn't stop running until she reached the edge of the academy's grounds. She glanced back at the castle with its sweeping stone towers and turrets. The first place she had truly been able to be herself. Now she would probably never see it again.

"Finally," Clarissa said. "I thought you had changed your mind."

"No, I stopped to call Lucas. If we wait a few minutes, he will be coming with us." She gasped for breath.

Clarissa gaped at her. "What? You didn't call him with your mind, did you?"

"Yes, why?" She frowned.

"Freya, Gerard can hear conversations in thought if they're close to him. He'll know!" Clarissa put a hand to her face. "We need to go through now before he comes after us." She grabbed Freya's arm.

"What? No, I'm not leaving without Lucas." She shook her head and pulled her arm free from Clarissa's grasp.

"Gerard is the most powerful fae around. He'll—"

Freya's heart pounded in her ears. How could she have been so stupid? She knew what Gerard's powers were. Yet she had been so desperate to get to Lucas, the thought hadn't even occurred to her that she might tip Gerard off.

"You should have listened to her." Gerard came up behind them. "What do you think you're doing, Goodwin?"

Clarissa shot in front of Freya. "We are leaving and there's not a damn thing you can do to stop us."

Gerard laughed. "You're not going anywhere so hand over the stone."

Clarissa tossed the stone to Freya. *Go through the portal. I'll be right behind you.*

"No!" Gerard threw a bolt of energy as Freya ran toward the portal.

Clarissa blurred out the way and Freya... The energy hit the standing stone behind her.

The stone in her hand pulsed with light as its magic flared to life. She hesitated. She didn't want to leave. Not without Lucas or Clarissa. What if something went wrong and they couldn't come through? She didn't want to be alone in the human world without them.

"What are you waiting for? Go!" Clarissa yelled.

Freya approached the standing stone. What if something happened to Clarissa? She would only be able to visit the Ever Realm on the solstice.

But Freya knew she couldn't let Gerard have the stone. She took a deep breath and stepped up to the standing stone.

The Everlight stone hummed, its light grew brighter as she headed straight through the portal. Light exploded around her. Energy reverberated through the air and seemed to tear apart the very fabric of space and time. Goddess, what had she done?

She hadn't considered what would happen to the stone if she tried taking it through the portal. Maybe the legends were true. Maybe this contained the very power of the Ever Realm itself.

She screamed as pain tore through her until everything

went black.

EPILOGUE

Freya's ears rang and her vision blurred. What happened? Had she got through to the human realm?

Her head ached and her throat felt dry. She opened her eyes, and it took several moments for her vision to clear.

"Freya?" Clarissa said. "You're awake. How do you feel?"

She blinked a few times and Clarissa came into focus. Freya now laid in a bed in an unfamiliar room. "I—I think so. Where are we?" The room had whitewashed walls with a pine wardrobe and chest of drawers. A fluffy rug covered the wooden floor and abstract art covered the walls.

"My mum's house. I came through the portal right after you." Clarissa put her hand on her stomach, which had become visibly rounder since Freya had last seen her.

"It worked? Are we in the human realm?" Her heart leapt.

"Yeah, but with a bigger problem. When you took the stone through parts of the Ever Realm came through to. The fae realm is falling apart now," Clarissa told her. "You've been unconscious for two weeks."

Freya frowned at her. "What? How is that possible?"

"My mum said the stone wasn't meant to leave the

Ever Realm. It broke in half and its power is inside you."

Freya put her head in her hands and moaned. "No, this can't be happening. Did I hurt anyone?"

How could the plan have gone so wrong? How could she have torn the entire realm apart? She didn't want to think about the kind of damage she had caused. One way or another, she had to find a way to fix it. If people had died because of her, she would never forgive herself. She knew she wouldn't be able to live with herself either.

"I'm not sure yet. Some of the humans were injured in places when the land shifted, but..." Clarissa shook her head. "You shouldn't blame yourself. We didn't know what would happen."

Freya wanted to wake up from this nightmare.

Clarissa turned on the TV and it was all over the news how parts of the human realm had disappeared. Different buildings now stood in their place.

"Where's the stone?" Freya said. "I will find a way to fix this."

"I doubt that will be possible." Clarissa pulled out the two broken halves of the stone. "This split when you went through."

Freya's mouth fell open. "What about Lucas? Where is he?"

"Still in the Ever Realm as far as I know. He wasn't in the academy when it passed over."

"There must be a way to fix this!" she cried.

"The stone doesn't have power anymore." Silantra, Clarissa's mother, came in. "The power of the Everlight is inside you. The stone is useless now." She was a tall woman with greying dark hair, dark blue eyes and an athletic build.

"I never meant for any of this to happen. If I have the power maybe I can use it to put the Ever Realm back together." She burst into tears and put her head in her hands.

"I wouldn't recommend using the magic again or you

could cause more devastation," Silantra replied. "And you would be putting your child at risk."

Freya's mouth fell open. "My what? I'm not—"

"It's very early, but I can sense it. You are pregnant. There's a chance your child may have the power too. The realms are in chaos now. You can never let anyone possess the power of the Everlight. If people find out where that stone's power went, your life, and your child's life will be in danger."

Freya shook her head. "I can't be pregnant. Lucas and I took precautions." She placed a hand on her stomach and cast her senses out. When she felt another presence, she almost recoiled.

She and Lucas had made love after they had said the joining vows. No wonder she had been feeling sick the past few days. She had put it down to stress. Not...

Clarissa took her hand. "Don't worry. We'll get through this together. I'm keeping my child. Together we will find a way to make this work."

Freya turned over and wept. One way or another, she had to find a way to fix this mess.

She wouldn't get rid of her child. But how could she keep it? If it had the power of the Everlight, what then?

Somehow, she would find her way back to Lucas. But would that even be possible now? She'd wait until she could find her way back to him, then decide what to do. After all, it was his child too.

THE END

Cursed Moon

CHAPTER 1

Clarissa Greenwood blurred to the edge of the woods. She couldn't believe Gerard, the Unseelie King, had found her again. After a year of being on the run, he had caught up with her. She should be home with her children, not running around between realms and blurring all over the place.

She stopped a moment to catch her breath. Fatigue weighed her down. The constant need to keep moving around and taking care of two babies had proved too much. At least her twins were safe with her mother.

She still didn't know how Gerard had found out about being their father. She had been relieved when he hadn't been interested in them.

No, he didn't want his children. He wanted something she had. It had been over a year since her best friend, Freya Goodwin, had found the Everlight stone—a source of power that kept the Fae Ever Realm in balance.

When she and Freya had left the Ever Realm to enter the human realm with the stone, disaster had struck. They had only fled to escape from Gerard. Or he would have used stone for his own nefarious purposes.

Clarissa and Freya had known little about the stone or

what it could do. Freya had discovered it a few days beforehand. When the stone had gone through the portal, it had been torn apart. Its power wrenched parts of the Ever Realm into the human one. Including the Everlight Academy where Freya had been staying. Since then, the Fae and humans had been forced to coexist together.

Her senses prickled in warning. Oh no, had he found her already?

Her mum had warned her not to leave the house, but Clarissa had to hide the other half of the stone. Freya had the other half and had hidden it somewhere safe.

Clarissa might not have been there when they found the stone, but she translated part of it. It had been her idea to bring it to the portal. She was just as much to blame for this whole mess as Freya.

She and Freya had agreed they could never let Gerard or Maeve, his girlfriend and the future Queen of the Seelie Court, use the stone. Or to find its missing power.

Gerard appeared out of the shadows. "Nowhere left to run, Clarissa," he growled. "Hand over the stone now and I just might let you go." He looked just as she remembered, with his dark hair and piercing blue eyes. Why she had thought him handsome enough to spend the night with him, she had no idea.

"How considerate of you," she sneered.

A drunken one-night stand with him had been the worst mistake of her life. That, along with the mess created by the stone. But at least she had got two beautiful babies out of it.

"I will never hand it over," she added. "You can chase me to the ends of the earth and the power of the Everlight will never be yours."

Gerard glowered at her. "If you don't, I'll take those children away from you."

Her hands clenched into fists. "You will never take Melanie or Tristen away. You said you didn't want them." She fought to keep her temper under control. He knew how to push your buttons better than anyone.

There was no way in hell she would let either of her kids grow up under his influence.

"Better than them growing up with you as their mother," he snapped. "Give me the stone. It belongs to me. I'm the one who found it."

That was untrue. Maeve, Freya and Freya's ex-boyfriend had also been there.

"Only a fae heir has the power to control it. That will never be you." Clarissa pulled the stone out of her jacket, traced runes with her free hand and threw it through a portal. As a Fey Guardian, she could open portals between different realms. "Now you'll never find it." She grinned and blurred away.

Gerard raised his hand. A bolt of energy shot through the air. Clarissa screamed as it went through her chest. She stumbled headlong into the lake mid-blur. Cold, icy water swallowed her up and hit her like a thousand tiny knives. Clarissa fought her way to the surface and gasped for breath.

Gerard stared down at her; his face devoid of all emotion. "Bring the stone back now or this place will be your grave."

Clarissa coughed and spluttered up water. She would die here. She had to get back to her children. To her mum. To tell Freya the stone would be safe now.

Gerard would never claim its power. How could he? The power transferred to Freya the moment she had stepped through the portal.

"Never," she choked out.

The water made it hard for her to use her speed. Instead, she swam to the edge of the lake. Tendrils of smoke swirled around her.

"You chose your own fate," Gerard growled, then vanished in a flash of light.

Clarissa gasped. The smoke choked her and wrapped around every fibre of her being. She called on her speed, but her legs gave out from under her. Her legs twisted and her body writhed in agony. Good goddess, she had seen death spells before but could never have imagined they would be this painful.

What had he done to her? Why hadn't she shielded herself?

Her mum always said her overconfidence in her abilities would be her undoing.

She had thought she was fast enough to get away.

Why had she even spoken to him? She should have run and kept going until she reached her mum's house. She'd only come here because it had been easy to open a portal close to the Academy. This was where the veil between the two realms had been torn.

All of those thoughts raced through her head. Her bones cracked and twisted.

Clarissa knew she had to do something. She drew magic to shield herself, but it was too low. Smoke curled around her even more like a serpent, cold and binding.

She could open the portal and get through. Maybe it would be enough to get Gerard's magic off her. She raised her hand and a swirling portal of energy enveloped her for a second, then faltered.

Her skin burned and her lower body twisted. She opened her mouth to scream, but no sound came out.

When she looked down, her legs and jeans had disappeared. Now replaced by a long silver fishtail. The scales extended to her upper torso and chest. Gills appeared on her neck. She couldn't breathe. The more she gasped for air, the more suffocated she felt. Clarissa crawled over to the edge of the lake. She couldn't believe Gerard had turned her into a bloody water fae.

She was a Fey Guardian, for crying out loud!

Had he meant to do this?

It didn't matter. She had to get to the water. Had to find a way to breathe again. The iciness enveloped her like a welcoming embrace. She breathed in through her gills and let out a long shuddering breath.

Damn Gerard.

She had spent the past two summers hanging out with him at Freya's Castle. He had called her water sprite due to her unusually strong swimming abilities. Now he turned her into a water fae. Which kind, she couldn't be sure. But she guessed it was probably a mermaid, judging by her tail.

Her legs were gone. Instead, she had to use her tail and fins to manoeuvre herself.

Damn you, Gerard!

One way or another, she would find a way to break whatever curse he'd used on her.

A few days passed. Clarissa got the hang of swimming and breathing underwater with her new alien body. So far, none of her attempts to get out of the lake had been successful. As soon as she got out of the water, she became unable to breathe. Her attempts to call her mum had failed, too.

Had she stopped being a Guardian?

She had learned to catch fish so she wouldn't starve at least. She had never been much of a fan of fish before and longed for some proper food again.

Someone had to be able to help her.

Clarissa wanted to call Freya, but she knew Freya was due to give birth any day now so she wouldn't be much help. Her attempts to open a portal hadn't worked either. Gerard might have cursed her, but she still had Guardian magic in her blood. So why wouldn't it work?

She swam around the depths of the lake as if she could find a way out.

"Clarissa?" someone called out her name.

Finally, after all the time waiting, someone had come to find her.

She cast her senses out. At least they still worked. She expected to sense Gerard or her mum.

Freya.

Her heart leapt.

Clarissa rushed to the surface. Freya stood a few feet away and gasped when she caught sight of Clarissa. "Good goddess!" She put her hand over her mouth. "What happened to you?" Freya was petite, pretty and had long blond hair with blue eyes. Her gossamer wings glittered on her back.

Clarissa opened her mouth and strange high-pitched sounds came out as she tried to speak.

Freya winced and clutched her ears. "I can't understand you."

Clarissa reached out to write in the dirt. Her webbed fingers refused to comply. She screamed with frustration.

Freya came over. "What happened?" She touched Clarissa's face.

"Gerard did it." She wanted to say, but the words wouldn't form. A tear dripped down her cheek. She wanted to tell Freya everything. To ask if her kids were okay.

"Gerard?" Freya guessed. "Did he do this?"

She nodded.

"How? Why would he?" Freya shook her head. "He came after the stone, didn't he? Goddess, I'm so sorry."

Clarissa motioned with her hands to signify a portal.

"You hid the stone?" Freya furrowed her brow.

She nodded.

"Is it safe?"

She nodded again.

Freya breathed a sigh of relief. "Good. Your mum and I have been worried sick about you. Your children are safe with her. Gerard hasn't come after them."

Clarissa motioned to Freya's now flat stomach. Where had her baby gone?

Freya bit back a sob. "I had a baby girl." she sniffed. "I left her among the humans."

Clarissa's mouth fell open. *Why would you do that?* She doubted Freya would hear her thoughts.

"You're wondering why, no doubt." Freya took a deep

breath. "I don't have the power of the Everlight anymore. All of it passed to her. I don't know why it happened. But I couldn't keep her. Gerard knew I had the power. No one but you and my sisters will ever know about my daughter." Tears streaked down her face. "Giving her up hurt so much. But it's the only way I can keep her safe from Gerard. I bound her powers so no one can trace the Everlight's power." She squeezed Clarissa's hand. "One way or another, I'll find a way to save you."

CHAPTER 2

18 years later

Clarissa swam around the lake as faint splinters of moonlight crested the water's surface. Finally, the blue ever moon had arrived at last. It only came once a year.

Freya usually came see her without fail to cast the spell that allowed Clarissa to change back into human form. It only lasted as long as the moon's light remained on the lake.

Clarissa breached the surface and spotted Freya running toward the lake. Her best friend looked ashen.

Freya chanted the spell and bright light blazed around Clarissa's body.

Her bones twisted and changed as she crawled onto land. Her gills faded and her scales changed into a shimmering blue dress of pure light. She took one long shuddering breath, then another.

"Freya…" Her voice sounded rough from disuse. Clarissa longed for this night every year she'd been trapped in that lake.

Gerard had come back a few times to demand answers, but Freya had cast a protection spell and forced the lake and a nearby river to connect. That way Clarissa could travel around and connect with other water fae.

That didn't stop her from longing for her old life and missing her family, though.

Freya seemed more on edge and kept glancing behind her. Like she expected someone to be there.

"What's wrong?" Clarissa asked. "You look anxious."

"We don't have much time." Freya sighed. "My daughter and your daughter, Melanie, both attend the academy now."

Clarissa gaped at her. "My Melanie? Why?"

"The council and the other Guardians got Gerard to back off."

"How? I sent it into the Ever Realm." Clarissa got to her feet and fell over on her unsteady legs. Walking always felt so alien to her now.

"I don't know. But Melanie's safe."

"What about Tristen?"

Learning the news Maeve had somehow adopted her son had devastated her. She couldn't imagine what he'd gone through growing up with that witch. Clarissa would have given anything to be there for both her children. But nothing they had tried so far had ended her curse.

"He's fine. He's grown up into a fine young man," Freya said. "My daughter is another matter. She has unbound her powers."

"What? Why?" Clarissa demanded. "You said keeping her bound was the only way to keep the Everlight's power hidden."

"She and Tristen somehow did it. Her powers were leaking out. I should have known I couldn't keep her bound forever." Freya ran a hand through her long blond hair. "Maeve is coming to see me tonight. No doubt to ask me about the stone. She's already suspicious enough of my daughter, Silvy."

"Why can't you bind her powers again?" Clarissa furrowed her brow.

Had her years of being cursed and everything she had

given up to protect that damn stone meant nothing?

"She's not a baby anymore. Her powers are too strong. I have no idea what to do about her or Maeve."

Clarissa crossed her arms. "Bring Maeve here and let me drown her. That would solve all their problems."

Freya shook her head. "Maeve is strong, but I have invited her here to talk."

"Why? Talking to her won't do any good." Clarissa couldn't believe Freya had been foolish enough to do such a thing. What good would talking do?

"I can't find any other way around Gerard's curse. If we hand over part of the stone, maybe it will be enough to get her to release you."

Clarissa uncrossed her arms and sat down on a log. "What will that achieve? She knows I'd fight like hell to get my son back."

"Tristen is of age now. Don't you want the chance to be your true self again? You need a monarch to do that. They're the only ones powerful enough to do that."

Clarissa sighed. "Of course, I want that! I don't understand why you would be so quick to give part of the stone away. We've spent years trying to prevent that from happening."

Her kids were almost adults now. She'd missed out on watching both of them grow up.

Freya ran a hand through her hair again. "I know. But I'm so tired of this. I'll find another way to bind some of these powers or to get the power out of her. I just want us to have a chance at normal lives again. To finally be with my child again." She paced up and down. "The stone has no power anymore. If it gives you your life back, then I'll do it. We've both lost enough already." Freya set her lips in a thin line. "I have my daughter back. It's time you got your children back to."

Maeve herself appeared in a flash of light. She looked as regal as ever in a designer black dress, with her glossy red hair and red lips. "Clarissa. Good goddess, I thought you were long dead."

Clarissa glowered at the fae queen. "As you can see, I'm not."

"We want to make a deal with you." Freya held out her broken half of the stone. "This, for changing Clarissa back and breaking Gerard's curse."

"Why would do I do that?" Maeve sneered. "You will try to take my son from me."

"Tristen is mine! I gave birth to him!" Clarissa snapped and her hands clenched into fists.

"You abandoned him and all because you didn't want Gerard and I to have that." Maeve motioned toward the broken shard of stone.

Clarissa scoffed. "Gerard would never have shared the Everlight's power with you and you know it."

"Enough!" Freya stepped in between them. "Clarissa won't do anything to Tristen, you have my word on that. If you release her, this half of the stone is yours."

Maeve's dark eyes narrowed. "What about the other half?"

"One half. That's all you get," Freya insisted.

Maeve hesitated. "How do I know that's the genuine stone?"

Freya held it up but didn't let go of it.

Maeve scrutinised it. "Very well. You have a deal, but I refuse to cast the counter curse out here. We can go back to the Academy and discuss this like civilised people."

"Cast the spell now," Freya demanded.

"Fine." Maeve scowled. "By the light of the moon and the powers that be, I release you from this curse, so you may now walk free."

Silver light enveloped Clarissa's body and washed over her like cool water.

"Now we'll go to my chambers at the Academy," Freya said. "All three of us. I have other terms too."

Maeve glowered at her but didn't object.

Clarissa breathed a sigh of relief, and the three of them

teleported back to the Academy.

She couldn't remember the last time she set foot inside an actual room. It felt like walking into a different world.

A world full of light and smells. The glow from the lamps stung her eyes and the smoke from the fire made her cough. Her eyes watered. Goddess, had being in human form always been this hard? It didn't matter. It felt good to be back in her true body again instead of being stuck under the lake.

"Sign this." Freya motioned to a piece of parchment on the table. "Sign it with your blood."

Maeve narrowed her eyes as she read through it. "You want me to stay away from Silvana?"

Clarissa stumbled, her legs still unfamiliar and wobbly.

"Yes, you need to back off and leave her alone," Freya snapped. "She might be a faeling but I'm her custodian."

Clarissa furrowed her brow. Why had Freya called her daughter a faeling? They both knew Freya's daughter was a full bloodied fae. And why had Freya become her custodian? She made a mental note to ask her about that later.

Clarissa sat down in one of the wingback chairs. Sitting felt even stranger than standing.

Silvana. Clarissa remembered how overjoyed Freya had been when she met her daughter again a year ago. Freya said she'd remained close to her but hadn't told her the truth about her parentage or anything else.

Clarissa wondered what her own kids looked like now. Freya said she kept watch on them, especially Tristen.

Maeve and Freya continued arguing. Freya even poured some tea.

Clarissa rose and caught sight of a photo on Freya's desk. Four teenagers sat together in the courtyard. A beautiful blond-haired girl who looked the spitting image of Freya sat at the centre of the table. That had to be Silvana. Next to her sat a dark-haired boy with electric blue eyes. Her heart lurched. Tristen.

Goddess, he looked so grown up. On the other side of the table sat a boy with dark hair, but the girl next to him caught her attention. Her long curly brown hair fell past her shoulders and she had the same blue eyes as her brother.

Melanie. This was her daughter. Goddess, both her children were so beautiful.

A tear dripped down her cheek.

"Either agree to my terms or I won't give you the stone," Freya snapped.

It brought Clarissa back to reality.

"Fine, I'll leave her alone," Maeve replied. "I know you're hiding something about her, and I will find out what it is."

"Maeve, just sign the damned parchment," Clarissa snapped.

"I will sign it if you swear you will make no claims on my son." Maeve arched an eyebrow and waited for Clarissa's response.

Clarissa opened and closed her mouth. She had lost all her parental rights to Tristen when Maeve had become his custodian.

What did it matter? Tristen was of age now. He couldn't be swayed by Maeve.

Freya gulped down some of her tea. "Just sign it, Clarissa."

"Fine, I'll do it." Clarissa picked up her tea and sniffed. Something didn't smell right about it. "Maeve, what did you put in this?"

Maeve grinned, screwed up the parchment and threw it into the fire. "No deal. I'll never give you anything."

Freya gasped and dropped her cup. "What have you done?"

"Simple. I added moon flower to your tea." She grabbed the stone.

Clarissa sank to her knees as pain tore through her. "You lied..."

114

"Of course, I did. You two have stood in my way long enough." Maeve laughed. "You will be dead soon enough, Freya." She turned to Clarissa. "And you can go back to your watery grave." She vanished in a flash of light.

Freya collapsed to the floor. "I'm—I'm sorry."

Despite the pain, Clarissa crawled over to her. "Never mind me. You're my best friend. You stood by me through everything."

"There will be no one… Left to protect Silvy…"

"I will watch her. I'll find a way." Clarissa clutched her hand.

In a flash of light, Clarissa found herself back in the dark depths of the lake.

CHAPTER 3

Months passed in the dull monotony of the lake. Travelling back and forth with the other water fae hadn't helped much either.

Often, she wanted to scream in frustration. Clarissa swam around the lake that night and spotted a strange blue light in the sky. She headed toward the surface to find out what happened.

Cool air stung her face as she breached the surface.

Something fell from the sky. It took a second to realise it was a girl with wings. Her body tumbled head over foot as she fell. More static shot over her body.

The Everlight's power. Good goddess, this must be Silvy.

Silvy screamed as she plunged into the water.

Clarissa dove back under. How had Gerard traced Silvy's power? Had Silvy done something to activate it?

It didn't matter. She knew she had to do something to suppress the power before Gerard located it. She swam over and grabbed hold of the girl. Good thing she hadn't lost any of her strength.

She dragged Silvy deeper and traced runes over her body. The runes flared with light to help Silvy breathe but not be affected by the water. Silvy struggled and fought against her.

It's okay, Silvy. I'm here to help you. Clarissa had no idea whether the girl would hear her since Freya couldn't communicate with her in thought either.

She pulled her down further. The deeper they got, the more the static subsided. Clarissa knew she would have to keep Silvy down there for a while to make sure Gerard's spell had worn off.

Once they reached the lake's bottom, she pulled Silvy into the wreck of a boat that she used for shelter. She expanded the bubble around Silvy and let her rest. Silvy's blond hair billowed around her face. She looked so much like Freya it made it almost painful to look at her.

Clarissa fumbled around for the bracelet she had seen Tristen toss into the lake a few days ago. She traced some runes over it for protection, healing and strength. The runes glittered with light as she slipped it onto Silvy's wrist.

You're safe now, Silvy, Clarissa told her.

She wished she could talk to the girl. Tell her everything, including the fact she had the power of the Everlight. Freya never had the chance to tell her before she died.

Clarissa raised her hands and the bubble around Silvy increased. She hoped it was enough to keep her alive. Even fae couldn't spend hours in freezing water.

Clarissa wondered what had happened to cause Gerard to come after her.

Wars between Silvy and Tristen?

She sensed someone near the lake. Had Gerard dared to enter her domain?

I'll be back soon, she said. *Get some rest.*

No way would she let him near that girl. She might not be able to help Freya anymore, but she could help Freya's daughter.

Clarissa swam out of the wreck and headed back toward the surface. Her heart fluttered with excitement. If Gerard had been foolish enough to come into the lake, she would drown him. It was no more than he deserved. Silvy and her kids would be safer then.

As she drew closer, she froze. Her mermaid body allowed her to see clearly in the dark.

Not Gerard, but Tristen.

Her son was close for the first time in eighteen years.

Tristen moved around the surface of the lake that she had covered with ice. She hadn't liked cutting him off, but she had no way to tell him she was trying to keep Silvy safe.

Clarissa wished she could reach out and touch him. Tell him how sorry she was for not being there for him.

After a few moments, he hit the surface of the ice again and continued to break through the top layer.

"Tristen?" Someone blurred over to the edge of the lake.

Good goddess, another Guardian. A woman with long, dark brown hair.

At first, Clarissa thought it might be Mel, but the woman looked to be in her late twenties. Though it was hard to tell with Guardians. Clarissa thought she and her mother were the last of their kind.

Tristen glanced over to her. "Silvy is missing now too. She fell in the lake! We were flying around trying to track Mel and she disappeared." Tristen gasped for breath. "The blue light. I lost contact with her."

"What were you even doing out here?" The other Guardian demanded. "You're supposed to be in the castle."

"Mel has been missing for weeks. You and Nick haven't found a single trace of her." Tristen ran a hand through his soaking wet hair.

Clarissa froze. Melanie had gone missing?

Goddess, if only Freya had been there to tell her.

"When did you last see Silvy?" The Guardian asked.

Tristen should his head. "A while ago. This was the last place I saw her, but I can't feel her anymore. Something

118

dragged her under and froze the entire like. What if something's happened to her?" He paced back and forth. "What the hell is in that lake?"

"We'll find a way to get through the ice. I promise we'll get her back."

"I can't feel her anymore. I always feel her!" Tristen turned and hit the ice with a blast of magic again. "I'll search this entire lake until I find her."

Clarissa dove back into the darkness.

Gerard had half of the stone and was no doubt close to finding the Everlight's power. She had to do something.

Silvy would be safe enough now. She had to find her daughter before Gerard realised Mel was of no use to him.

Clarissa swam upstream to the river that connected to the lake. She flung her senses out like a net. Where would Gerard have taken Mel?

That Guardian said they had already searched his compounds.

They probably didn't know about the summer Castle close to the Academy, though. It had been his secret place. He hadn't even told Maeve about it from what she remembered.

Clarissa swam further up the river. Gerard's Castle lay beyond a wall of energy.

Mel's presence came through to her.

She had to find a way to get help to her before it was too late.

Silvy passed in and out of consciousness all night. Tristen and the others had searched for her and kept trying to break through the ice.

Clarissa knew she couldn't keep the girl down there any longer. Silvy needed air and heat to recover from her injuries, otherwise she would drown. Clarissa dragged Silvy from the wreck and back towards the surface. It took some manoeuvring.

A high-pitched screech tore through the air and the ice

broke apart. That ice should have been impenetrable to any magic but her own.

She sensed another presence and spotted Tristen a few feet away sat under a tree with his head in his hands.

Her heart clenched. She realised he must love her very much. She hated to see her son hurting.

Clarissa grunted as she dragged Silvy onto dry land.

Silvy remained unconscious. Clarissa couldn't find a pulse either. Crap, she kept the girl down there for too long.

Silvy needs help! She splashed around to get his attention.

Tristen looked up. "Silvy?" He raced over and stared at Clarissa. "Who hell are you?"

"I'm your mother." She wanted to say but couldn't. She might scare him with her high-pitched wails. She motioned to Silvy and mouth the word "help".

Tristen leaned down and checked for a pulse. "She's not breathing." He started chest compressions.

You'll be alright, son, Clarissa told him and sank back under the water. *You'll find a way to save her and your sister.*

Then maybe, she'd be free from this curse at last.

The end

Wings of Fate

CHAPTER 1

The walls of her tree house trembled and Alia's heart pounded in her ears. *Goddess, what's happening?* She wondered and stumbled. It reminded her of what happened eighteen years ago when parts of the Ever Realm had fallen into the human world.

Could that happen again? She had only been five at the time. Her mother had promised she would never have to endure that again and insisted their home would be safe. But more parts of the Ever Realm fell away every day. How much more would go into the human world before this realm disappeared into oblivion?

People started running and screaming as they fled from their homes.

Alia knew she had better get to safety too. But first she had to find her life mate, Declan.

He would be out working in the forest. Maybe he would come back to look for her. He'd be just as concerned as she was.

She hurried down the steps from the tree house and glanced over at several people who were headed in the opposite direction. "Declan?" she called out. "Has anyone seen Declan?"

No one bothered to reply.

She grabbed hold of a man as her panic grew. "Where is Declan?"

The man shoved her away. "How should I know? We have to get out of here before we all die!" He ran off without saying another word.

Alia carried on running. Above her, the usual neon blue sky had turned purple. She knew time was running out. She had to find Declan so they could get to safety. But where would they even go? If their realm fell away, no one would be able to stop it. All they could do was pray to the goddess and hope they came out the other side. Wherever that may be.

It would take too long to cover the entire forest on foot. Alia unfolded her gossamer wings and took to the air. Energy sizzled against her skin as the light overhead grew brighter.

Where would Declan be? She knew he spent most of the morning cutting wood that was used to build their homes and for other purposes. So she scanned forest with her mind, but her senses had never been good at tracking people. It wasn't her gift.

Alia swooped lower as a dark cloud rolled over the treeline like smoke. That couldn't be good. Everything inside her screamed in warning to get away from the darkness. But how could she leave Declan behind? If something bad happened to him she would never forgive herself. She wouldn't leave until she found him. Even if it meant being swept up by the cloud.

Alia darted through the trees, scanning everything in sight. "Declan?" she called out. "Declan, where are you?" She still couldn't anything through the static of the oncoming storm.

Goddess, please protect my home, she prayed. *Don't let it disappear.*

The Ever Realm had barely survived the last eighteen years. Fae had either disappeared or were presumed dead.

Forced to make their new home in the human realm.

"Declan?" She dove lower and called out for him again. He had to be here somewhere. "Declan, where are you?" Fear gripped her like icy fingers.

Finally, she spotted someone up ahead. Her heart leapt. "Declan?" She landed and ran toward the figure. Her long pink hair billowed around her face and she caught hold of the hem of her long dress as she ran.

The man turned and she froze. He had long black hair, icy blue eyes, and wore a sneer.

The Unseelie King.

"This—this isn't your part of the Ever Realm," she stuttered. "These are Seelie parts. You're not supposed to be here…"

The king raised his hand, and a blast of invisible energy knocked her to the ground.

Alia winced. "Forgive me." She bowed her head. She knew better than to disrespect a monarch.

"Haven't you heard? The Seelie Queen has been imprisoned. What little that remains of her realm now belongs to me," King Gerard said. "You're a healer, aren't you?"

She nodded but kept her mouth shut. Alia didn't want to offend him further.

"Good. If you want your husband back, then you will do everything I tell you to."

Alia looked up, her blue eyes wide. "Declan? What have you done with him?" All her fear subsided.

"He's somewhere safe but you won't get him back until you've done a job for me."

"I want to see him!" Her hands clenched into fists. "We are Seelie folk. You have no right to—" Alia aghast as Gerard raised his hand. An invisible noose wrapped around her neck and cut off her air. She choked and gasped for breath. Her lungs burned, and she still couldn't draw in air.

"Listen to me. Your Queen is gone. No one sits on the

Seelie throne now."

"Her son…" She barely choked the words out.

"*My* son hasn't taken the throne. He'd make a poor leader, anyway." The king gave a harsh laugh. "Now, will you behave, or should I just kill you?"

Alia bobbed her head and gasped when the tightness around her throat faded. "What… What do you want with me?" Her heart pounded in her ears so hard she thought it would burst through her chest.

What could he possibly want from her? She was a healer. No one special. She wasn't powerful and couldn't do anything for him. Why would he take Declan? He didn't have much power either.

"I have a job for you."

The rolling cloud of darkness swallowed everything around them. Trees vanished as it continued to sweep through the forest like an oncoming tidal wave, consuming everything in its wake.

The king held out his hand to her. "Come."

Alia hesitated. If she went with this man, what would she have to do? Even if she did as he asked that didn't guarantee she would see Declan again. The Unseelie were considered dark fae. Untrustworthy and evil in their intentions.

The Seelie were light fae, good and beloved by the goddess. The darkness swept further. It swallowed the trees, birds and everything else in its wake. If she stayed, she might end up somewhere else. Or she might die. Either way she wouldn't see Declan again.

Alia took a deep breath and grasped the king's hand.

She blinked as bright sunlight dazzled her. The sky shone blue without a cloud in sight. No rolling darkness appeared. Birds sang and a yellow stone castle stood a few feet away.

"Where are we?" she asked and raised her hand to shield her eyes from the brightness.

"The Goodwin estate. Home to the former leaders of

the spring court," the king informed her. "This is where I have a job for you. Go to the castle and tell them how your home got destroyed by the darkness. They'll ask you questions, and you will answer them as truthfully as you can. But you will give them no reason to suspect you. Nor will you tell anyone I sent you here or your husband will die."

She furrowed her brow. "I don't understand. Do you expect me to kill someone?" She had sworn her life to helping others. She couldn't take a life even she wanted to. Alia knew she wouldn't be able to live with herself if she did such a thing.

The king gripped her hand, and they appeared in a large bedroom with blue-coloured walls and a plush cream carpet. In a large double bed lay a woman with long blond hair. "This is Freya Goodwin, heir to the spring court. Or at least she was. Now I possess her soul," Gerard stated. "This is the woman responsible for bringing the Ever Realm into the human world. She destroyed our beloved homeland."

Alia's eyes widened. "What do you expect me to do?" She wondered if he wanted her to heal Freya. She couldn't be sure, but judging by the look of Freya's body, she was beyond saving.

"Convince Goodwin firmly to let you become Freya's live-in healer. Freya stole a valuable artefact from me and I need to get it back before the rest of the Ever Realm falls into oblivion. You will stay here. Watch everything her family does, especially her daughter, Silvana. She is the key to finding what I need." He held out a black crystal. "Use this to make your reports."

The idea of her spying on people sounded so ridiculous she almost laughed. But she kept her mouth shut to avoid angering him. How could she spy on anyone? Alia spent her days gathering herbs and helping people. Not watching everything they did. She didn't know the first thing about being a spy.

"I'm a healer. How do you expect me to spy on these people?"

"If you want to get Declan back, you will get me what I need." The king vanished in a flash of light.

Alia blew out a breath. One way or another, she needed to find a way out of this mess.

CHAPTER 2

Two months had passed. The Goodwin family questioned her story when she told them she fled from the Ever Realm but had welcomed her. Freya's sisters, Elsa and Zenia, had been nothing but kind.

For the most part, she remained alone in the guesthouse with Freya and took care of her. She still found it strange taking care of a body whose soul was stuck somewhere between life and death.

The sisters had told her to keep Freya comfortable. Every time they came to visit, they seemed to expect Freya to be gone. They also told her there was no chance of Freya's soul arriving. She had been comatose for over eight months.

Alia watched the sisters as much as she could but had yet to meet Freya's daughter.

The king grew more impatient with her every day. But staying in the guesthouse meant she didn't get to see that much of the Goodwin family. She rarely got to see anyone up at the castle. She could only make so many excuses to go there. The sisters were kind enough to let her have dinner there until recently. They told her people would be staying at the castle and asked her not to come there unless it was an emergency.

Alia had snuck up there again that morning and got a glimpse of four teenagers. She realised one of them must be Freya's daughter.

Silvana looked so much like her mother. They had the same slim build, blue eyes and long blond hair.

Alia edged closer. If she could hear what they were saying, she might finally have some news to share with the king.

She missed Declan more every day.

Silvana played around in a pool with a girl with long curly brown hair and a dark-haired boy. They laughed and splashed each other with water.

Alia realised how much she longed to be around people again. She got so lonely being in the guesthouse. Although she felt grateful to the Goodwin's for allowing her to stay and giving her money.

From what she'd heard, other people escaping from the Ever Realm hadn't been so lucky. Now they lived as refugees.

Alia wondered what the king would do if she didn't get what he needed. Would she ever see Declan again? Was he even alive? And if so, where was he?

She had considered asking the Goodwin's to help but realised it wouldn't do any good. They were no match for the Unseelie King.

And it wouldn't change anything. If the king could steal Freya's soul, what chance did anyone else have against him?

"Come on, Alec, catch!" The brunette girl threw a large inflatable ball at him.

Alec caught hold of it. "What's this for?" He frowned.

"You're supposed to throw it." The girl rolled her eyes. "Toss it to Silvy."

Alia leaned closer. Why couldn't they mention something about the stone? Or say something she could pass along to the king?

"Hey, what are you doing?" Another voice caught her off-guard.

A young man with short black hair, piercing blue eyes and a chilling face stared at her. He was naked from the waist up and wore blue shorts.

"I—" Alia struggled to find the right words.

She could get in so much trouble over this. Both with the Goodwin's and the king. What if they told her to leave? How would she ever find Declan then?

So, she did the only thing she could think of. She ran. Her heart pounded in her ears as she sprinted away. Once she reached the gardens, she unfurled her wings and flew off.

Alia didn't stop until she reached the guesthouse. Once inside, she closed the front door behind her and let out a breath she had been holding. *Stupid, stupid.*

She should have been more careful. But then again, how else would she overhear anything whilst stuck in this house all day?

Alia headed back to the bedroom. "That was close," she murmured to Freya.

Since she had no one else to talk to she often spoke to Freya. What else could she do? A one-sided conversation felt better than talking to herself all the time.

"You'll be pleased to know your daughter is here, Freya. She looks so much like you." Alia gave her a faint smile.

The front door opened and the dark-haired boy she had seen earlier strolled in. "Who are you?" he demanded. "Why are you spying on—?" He gasped. "Freya."

Alia fell to her knees. Only a fool wouldn't recognise the fae prince. This was Tristen, the son of Queen Maeve and King Gerard. She hadn't expected to see him here of all places. "My Prince."

"How is she still alive?" Tristen demanded. "Who are you?"

"I'm Alia. I'm a survivor of the Ever Realm," she said

in a small voice. "I'm a healer—I look after Freya."

Elsa Goodwin came in and gasped. "Tristen, what are you doing in here? You're not supposed to be here."

Alia shrank back. She would get into so much trouble for this! Her mind raced as she tried to come up with an excuse, but nothing sounded plausible enough to explain why she had been up at the castle. Why hadn't she been more careful?

Tristen spun to face her and narrowed his eyes. "Why are you letting Silvy believe her mother is dead?"

"Tristen, Alia is here to take care of Freya until she passes. Her body is only still alive because of a spell Madame Leticia cast on her," Elsa said. "There's no hope of saving Freya, which is why you can't tell Silvy about this."

"What?" Tristen gaped at her. "I can't keep something like this from her. She's my girlfriend."

Elsa shook her head. "Silvy has been through so much. Losing Freya devastated her. Do you want to put her through that again?"

Alia slipped out the room. She hated feeling like an intruder, but at least she had seen Silvana at last. She just had no idea what to do with the information. But she wouldn't tell the girl the truth about her mother. It wasn't her business.

If the Goodwin family decided to send her away, where else could she go?

Tristen left the house a few moments later. Their eyes met.

Alia flushed and wondered what she should do.

"You came through from the Ever Realm?" he asked her.

She nodded, unsure what to say. Goddess, did he suspect she was a spy? Or perhaps paranoia had got the better of her.

"You ended up here?" Tristen arched an eyebrow.

"Yes." She tucked a lock of her hair behind her ear.

"I'm a healer so the family offered me a place to live and work."

"Most of the fae who came through recently came out near the academy."

Alia took a step back and tried to regain her composure. She had heard the Prince had the same powers of compulsion that his father had. If he used his power on her, she would have no choice but to tell him the truth. Somehow, she knew that wouldn't make the king very happy and would only make him punish her further.

"Not everyone comes out at the same place," she pointed out. "I went back into the forest to find my husband. Then... I came here."

Tristen still stared at her, making her shift from foot to foot.

"Are you going to tell your girlfriend the truth?" She decided averting the attention from herself would be better.

Besides, she wasn't here to hurt anyone. Only to watch like the king said. If he had told her to harm someone she would never have agreed to stay. Not even to get Declan back.

Tristen flinched. "I—I don't know."

"There is no hope of Freya being saved. I'm surprised she has lasted this long."

"I'm not sure if I can keep this from Silvy. She's been through so much already." His expression grew pained.

"Sometimes we have to do whatever it takes to protect the people we love," she said. "Even if it means them getting hurt."

Tristen nodded and walked off without saying another word.

CHAPTER 3

Alia knew time was running out. Another month had passed, and she had learnt nothing to tell the king. She had been up to the castle and spied on Silvy a few times but heard nothing useful. She had come close to getting caught more than once, but always made an excuse whenever anyone spotted her.

Elsa had asked her not to come up to the gardens or the castle unless it was necessary. She said it was because she didn't want Silvy to know the truth about her mother.

Alia was losing her mind being stuck in the guesthouse all the time. So, she started offering her services to people in the nearby village. Helping others at least made her feel useful, and the Goodwin's hadn't objected to her doing that.

She cared for Freya that morning and made sure she was bathed and clean. Then she checked to make sure her feeding tube and groups were in.

The king appeared in a flash of light. "Why aren't you getting the information I need?" he demanded. "It's been weeks now, and you have given me nothing. What have you been doing all day? I doubt it's that hard taking care of a half dead body."

Alia jumped and bowed her head. "I—I'm performing my duties here."

"Your duty is to get me information. That girl has spent months here, and you did nothing?"

"I tried my best. I'm a healer, not a trained spy," she snapped. "I'm sick of this."

"You're not trying hard enough." Gerard glowered at her. "Don't you want to see your husband again? He's not having a very pleasant time rotting away in my dungeon. He calls out for you a lot."

Alia flinched at that. She hated to think of the kind of suffering Declan might be going through. "I'm doing my best. The Goodwin's have been nothing but kind to me. I hate having to spy on them so much."

"Do you want your husband to die?"

"How do I even know he's alive?" She put her hands on her hips. "I haven't seen him since the day you took him."

"He's alive, you have my word on that. You will find something about my stone, or he won't be for much longer." The king vanished in a flash of light.

Alia blew out a breath. "What am I going to do?"

A couple of days passed. She didn't have many healing duties, so she sat in the living room to read through some of Freya's journals. She had found them during a visit to the castle and had smuggled them out. Maybe she'd find something in there about the elusive stone the king wanted.

The door burst open and Silvy herself stormed in.

Alia jumped up in alarm and shoved the journal she had been reading down the side of the armchair.

"Where's my mother?" Silvy demanded.

Alia opened her mouth, but no words came out. She didn't want to be the one to have to tell Silvy about Freya.

Silvy stormed past her when she didn't get a response.

Alia shook her head to clear it and pulled herself together. She had no idea how Silvy had found out about

Freya being here.

Tristen came in a few moments later and gave her a guilty look. Perhaps he had told Silvy the truth. "Sorry," he muttered as he hurried past her. Although she didn't know what he had to apologise for.

Alia shoved the other journals under the coffee table. She knew she shouldn't have them, but what choice did she have? She had to do something to get the king the answers he needed. Whenever she went back to the castle, she put a journal back after she had read through it. That way she hoped no one would notice they had gone missing.

She crept down the hall and heard the couple arguing.

"We're done," Silvy said. "Get out!"

Tristen walked out; face drawn as he headed past her.

Alia didn't want to intrude, but one of her duties was to watch Freya. So, she headed inside the bedroom to find Silvy staring at her mother at her bedside. "I'm sorry you had to find out like this," Alia said. "I'm the healer assigned to watch her."

Silvy narrowed her eyes. "Was it your idea to keep this a secret?"

Alia flinched, surprised by the girl's hostility. "No, of course not. Freya was like this long before I came here. Your aunts hired me to watch her until she... Until it's time." Alia swallowed hard. "She's been like this since the day she was poisoned. Her body lives but her soul is gone."

Silvy bit back sob. "There must be something you can do. Why can't you heal her?"

Alia put her hand on Silvy's shoulder. "That's beyond my power. Someone else has her soul—at least that's what I've heard. I'm so sorry, but at least now you know. Now you will have a chance to say goodbye to her."

Silvy shoved her hand away and glared at her. "If the king has her soul, I'll find a way to stop him. Please leave me alone."

Alia winced. Had she said something wrong?

She left and called Elsa. Perhaps it would be better for her family to explain the situation to Silvy.

After that, Silvy came to the guesthouse every day to visit her mother. Sometimes in the early morning, other times in the evening. But at least it gave Alia an excuse to watch over her. Most of the time she just sat and talked to Freya. Other times she sat there reading.

Alia peered around the doorway and caught Silvy crying.

Her heart ached for the girl. She cried most nights because she missed Declan so much. So, she decided to go and see if she was okay. "Are you alright?" Alia asked.

Silvy sniffed. "No, I broke up with my boyfriend. My friend is missing—the king took her," she said, her voice thick. "Everyone around me keeps lying to me. I don't know what to do anymore."

Alia decided to make them some tea. "Here," she said. "You look like you need a break."

"I can't find a way to save Freya either." Silvy slumped onto the seat next to the fireplace. "I don't understand why someone can't get her soul away from Gerard."

"The king is a powerful man." Alia sat down in the opposite seat. "I doubt anyone can stop him from getting what he wants."

"Is that why you're still here?" Silvy asked. "Because he's taken something from you?"

Alia gaped at her. "No, I... I don't know what you mean."

"I know Gerard sent you here to spy on me. He wants to find the stone." Silvy pushed her tea away. "There's no point in lying. I'm an aura reader. I spotted you watching me and my friends over the summer too."

"I—" Alia put her head in her hands and burst into tears. "I'm so sorry! He took my husband. I didn't have a choice but to stay here or the king will kill him!"

Silvy reached out and touched her arm. "It's okay. I

know you don't mean any harm. If you did, I wouldn't be here talking to you."

"I don't know what to do," she moaned. "My husband could be dead, and I wouldn't know it."

"Then I'll help you find him. If you need me to."

Alia stared at her in disbelief. "How? If I turn against the king—"

If she turned against Gerard, he would kill her and Declan. He had only chosen her because he thought she would be useful to him.

"You're going to feed him information and carry on as normal. And you're going to help me find him."

***

Over the next few weeks, Silvy somehow managed to revive her mother. Alia still wasn't sure how she had managed to do such a thing. It should have been impossible. Yet over the coming days Freya seemed to make a full recovery. Another healer had come to check on her and confirmed Freya wasn't being possessed by another spirit, and she had indeed returned.

Now that Freya no longer needed Alia to care for her, she was offered a position as a healer at the Academy. It had overwhelmed her at first having to deal with so many people, but she soon grew to love the role.

Eventually Silvy became the new fae queen and Declan was returned to her.

The end

The Darkest Touch

CHAPTER 1

Kristina Dixon couldn't wait to see her fiancé, Jake, to tell him the good news. She had finally been offered a place at Everlight Academy as a history and magical arts teacher. Jake would call her insane taking on double work since she'd be teaching two different classes, but opportunities like this didn't come along very often.

The academy had a new headmaster, and there had been a big shakeup going on in the fae world. The Seelie Queen, Maeve, had been sent to prison. Some said because she had tried to kill her son's girlfriend, and that the Unseelie King had somehow been involved. Kris couldn't care less about the fae royals' drama. She just wanted to tell her fiancé her big news.

Lucas Melrose had been pretty nice for a fae. Completely unlike Forrest Thornwood, the former headmaster, who'd been a misogynistic pig. Forrest had never given her the time of day. Even though they both knew she had the qualifications necessary to teach at the academy.

She hurried through the streets of Colchester. Cars beeped and whooshed past her as she headed through the high street. Her long silver and purple hair whirled around her as she headed toward Castle Park. Colchester Castle loomed up ahead. The place always gave her a weird feeling. She had no idea why, though.

Kris glanced at her watch. Jake had promised to meet her here. It wasn't like him to be late. She sat down on the bench and checked her phone. No missed calls or messages appeared.

She tapped her foot. She wanted to get home and celebrate. Why hadn't Jake shown up yet? Was he late or had something held him up? She wondered if she should call him, but then she'd probably spill the beans about her job.

Kris checked her phone again. Smoke whirled around and the outline of a skull appeared. Good goddess, what was that? Kris' heart jumped and pounded in her ears. As a witch with fae blood, she often worked with spirits but had never seen anything like that.

A woman with long dark purple hair, dark eyes and wearing a purple dress with white and purple striped tights, appeared and grinned at her.

"Lily," Kris gasped. "Is that you?"

Lily had been a fellow witch from her coven who'd been killed over a year ago. Kris had tried to summon her spirit several times but had never been successful. It had always struck her as odd because Kris knew Lily better than anyone. Lily would have wanted revenge for her death.

"Hey, Kris, long time no see." Lily grinned.

She frowned. "You don't look like a spirit." Working with spirits was part of her power. It was what had helped her get her new job too.

Most supernaturals didn't know how to handle spirits or interact with them.

"I became a banshee after I died thanks to my fae blood," Lily explained. "Now I'm a reaper." She held up her hand when Kris opened her mouth to speak. "Long story. I found the guy who was responsible for killing me.

Actually, it turned out to be a stupid accident." She rolled her eyes. "I would have thought my death would have had more meaning somehow. But that's not why I've come."

"Okay, why are you here?"

Part of her was glad to see her friend again. They had been close before Lily died.

Lily hesitated and Kris realised she hadn't stopped by for a visit.

"It's not my time to die, is it?" Her heart skipped a beat.

She'd been so excited about her new job and planning the wedding she hadn't considered it might be her time. If so, it wasn't fair. She had her whole life ahead of her and wasn't ready to give it up.

Lily shook her head. "Not for you. Your soul is safe, don't worry. I came to warn you about Jake. It's his time to die, so I thought you'd want the chance to say goodbye."

All colour drained from her face. "What? When is this supposed to happen?" she demanded. "Why? He's too young to die!"

"Kris, death is a part of life. You know that. There's not always a reason why," Lily told her. "I don't know how or when it will happen. I just wanted to give you a heads up."

"That's not true. Reapers can see glimpses of deaths," Kris snapped. "Tell me how it happens!"

"Kris—"

"Lily, you can't come and tell me my fiancé is about to die and expect me not to do anything." Her hands clenched into fists. "We will find a way to stop this from happening."

"You know better than anyone you can't stop death when it's someone's time. That's the natural order of things. Most people never get a chance to say goodbye."

"Please, tell me!" Kris gripped her friend's shoulder, surprised when she made contact with solid flesh.

Lily sighed. "There's some kind of wolf involved.

141

That's all I know. You should go and find him."

Kris swung her bag over her shoulder. "Thanks." She ran off in the opposite direction.

"But don't try to stop it," Lily called after her. "You know you can't!"

Kris ignored the warning. As she ran across the town toward home, she tried calling Jake several more times. His phone went straight to voicemail.

Damn it, why wouldn't he answer? Had something already happened?

He'd already missed their meeting at the park.

When she reached the door of their block of flats, she hurried up the steps and flung the front door open.

"Jake?" she yelled. "Jake, are you here?"

No answer came.

Lily tried his phone again and screamed when she heard the voicemail message.

Why wouldn't he answer?

Her mind raced as she figured out her next move.

Jake would have left work by now. He worked as a tracker. Trackers worked security jobs and hunted fugitives. Sometimes he turned his phone off when he worked, but he usually called or texted to let her know if he was going to be late.

Where had he said he'd be working today?

She had been so nervous about her interview she couldn't remember. Why hadn't she listened more? If she hadn't been so focused on her interview, she would know where he was.

Instead, Kris pulled out a map of the town and a drowsing crystal, along with one of his T-shirts. She held the crystal over the map and it swayed back and forth.

A few seconds later it dropped over Castle Park.

Kris furrowed her brow. Had he been at the park the whole time?

In her mad rush to get home, she might have run right past him.

She chanted a spell to transport herself. She didn't have time to run all the way back there. Kris reappeared back near the bench where she had sat earlier. The park spread out before her. There were coloured flower beds, steep sweeping paths and birds flying about.

Jake couldn't be here, could he?

"Jake?" Kris called out. "Jake, are you here?" She glanced around and noticed how quiet it had become.

The park never got this quiet. There were always people around. Dog walkers, people on bikes and people with kids.

Her senses prickled in warning. A growling sound came from somewhere in the nearby woods. Kris took off after the sound.

Damn, why hadn't she thought to bring some sort of weapon with her?

Stupid, stupid! Leaves crunched under her boots as she hurried after the noise.

Up ahead blood covered the grass. Her heart stopped. A few feet away lay a pile of torn and shredded clothes. Jake's clothes. Along with his phone and other belongings.

Her heart twisted at the sight. "Oh, goddess." She fell to her knees.

Could Jake have somehow survived that kind of blood loss? But if his clothes were here, where was his body?

Tears stung her eyes as she wondered if she would ever see him again.

CHAPTER 2

Two months had passed. Jake's death had been ruled an accident by an animal attack.

Kris had scoffed at that. Yeah, right! This was England. The only large animals they had here were shifters. But most of them lived on an island near Cornwall.

She couldn't believe he'd died. She wouldn't believe it. But after no one had found his body, everyone, both human and supernatural alike, insisted she needed to accept he was gone. But she refused to believe that.

If he was dead, why hadn't she seen his spirit?

She tried to summon him every day since he had disappeared, but he had never come to her. Then again, if he was alive, why hadn't he come back to her? He wouldn't leave her without good reason. Or at least she didn't think he would.

Some people said he got cold feet, but she didn't believe that either.

Kris sighed and wondered if she should have turned down the job. She had spent the last few weeks searching for Jake instead of preparing for her new position. She didn't feel prepared at all as she stared at the yellow stone walls of the castle with its towers and turrets. It looked like something out of a fairy-tale.

Her initial excitement over her new job had faded the moment Jake had gone missing.

She took a deep breath and let it out. Her heels clicked as she headed up the sweeping gravel path to the academy's main entrance. Goddess, could she even do this?

Get your bum in there and show them how brilliant you are, Jake's voice whispered in her mind.

Kris froze for a moment. She felt his presence nearby. She spun, and half expected to see him there. But found no one.

Had he been there? Or had it been wishful thinking?

Kris scanned the area with her senses and found no trace of Jake. Why had she heard his voice? She wished he was there. She would give anything just to see him again, and tell him how much she missed him. Kris missed talking to him. Missed waking up next to him.

She stood and stared for a while, but no one appeared. Maybe it had been wishful thinking. She hadn't sensed a spirit nearby either.

Kris took another deep breath and headed up the steps and through the gateway to the academy.

The hallway opened up with suits of armour and rich tapestries hanging on the walls. Along with different plaques, commemorating various head teachers who had served the academy over the years.

The place looked similar to a medieval castle despite being a school. Kris still reeled from hearing Jake's voice. How she wished she knew if it had been real or not. She wished she had a chance to look around or cast a spell to find out if it had been Jake. But she couldn't afford to be late on her first day, that wouldn't make her look very professional.

Kris headed down the hall, surprised at seeing no students milling about.

Maybe that was good. She didn't know how the fae

kids who attended the academy would react to her. Just because there was a new headmaster didn't mean fae attitudes toward witches had changed.

She took another deep breath as she reached the headmaster's office door and knocked.

The door opened a few moments later. Lucas Melrose looked the same as she remembered. Bookish, yet handsome with dark hair and blue eyes. He wore a rumpled dark suit, blue shirt and a tie. Very unlike the immaculate man Forrest Thornwood had been. But Kris didn't mind. Lucas seemed a much nicer guy than Forrest had ever been.

"Oh, Kristina, sorry I'm a bit scattered," Lucas said. "Come in, come in." He motioned her into the room.

Kris took a seat in the uncomfortable skinny visitor's chair. "I can't wait to get started." She spotted a photo on the desk of Lucas with a blond haired young woman.

"Yes, I've got the schedule around here somewhere." Lucas looked over his desk. "Goddess, Forrest left this place in such chaos when he stepped down. I still don't understand why they chose me."

"I'm sure you'll manage just fine." Kris gave him a reassuring smile.

Lucas rummaged through the piles of paper and knocked the photo over in the process.

Kris caught hold of it. "She's a pretty-looking girl."

Lucas took the photo and gave a genuine smile. "She is. She is my daughter, Silvana. I still can't quite believe I'm a father."

She frowned. "What do you mean?"

"I only found out about her a few months ago. Her mother didn't tell me about her until..." Lucas shook his head. "Silvy is a student here. You'll meet her when classes begin tomorrow."

"Really, what's she like?"

"Strong, very stubborn and wilful. Opinionated too, but I can't imagine life without her now." Lucas laughed.

146

"Don't let the students intimidate you. They are still children."

The academy taught kids from the ages of fourteen to eighteen. Kris couldn't deny being nervous about that. The kids she would be teaching would be final-years. Kids who were almost adults.

Lucas finally found the schedule, then gave her a tour of the classrooms and other parts of the academy. Kris found it fascinating, but her mind kept wandering back to Jake.

"These are your chambers." Lucas led her up to the top floor of the castle. "There is a bedroom, bathroom, small kitchen area and living area. Most of the staff usually eat in the great hall with the students."

"I'm sure it'll be fine, thanks."

Kris dropped her bag on the desk.

The room didn't have much. A couple of chairs, a bookcase and a table with two chairs.

She still had her flat back in Colchester but working here for the next few months meant she had to live on site too.

Kris didn't mind. It felt better than being cooped up in a flat all day. Maybe she could do more to find Jake here. This place had a wealth of knowledge.

Lucas left her and Kris got to work unpacking her stuff.

She set up a spell circle and lit several candles. Then she chanted a spell to take her to Jake. She waited as the familiar rush of magic went through the room.

Nothing else happened.

Kris gritted her teeth in frustration. She tried a tracking spell instead, but that did nothing either.

Later that evening Kris awoke to the sound of a wolf howling.

She turned the lamp on and screamed when she spotted Lily in the corner.

"Geez, you make enough noise to wake the dead!" Lily

groaned. "The dead do sometimes wake up, you know."

Kris put her hand to her chest to steady her pounding heart. "Christ, Lily, what are you doing?"

"Just checking on you." Lily crossed her arms and leaned back against the wall. "Can't a friend be concerned about you?"

"You're like death itself. Reapers don't check on people." Kris kicked her duvet off and ran a hand through her damp hair.

"I still watch other people who I care about." Lily glanced around. "This is EverLight Academy. Cool, you always wanted a job here."

"Why are you here?"

"I need your help with something. Do you remember my foster kid Silvy? She goes here."

"Lily!" Kris stared at her. "Get to the point, damn it!"

"Can't a friend come and wish you good luck with your new job?" Lily tried to look innocent.

Kris scowled. "Subtlety has never been one of your traits."

"Fine, I have a favour to ask. Can you keep an eye on my kid?"

She frowned and rubbed sleep from her eyes. "You don't have a kid."

"One of my foster kids that I used to work with. Her name is Silvana Eldry."

"Silvana? You mean the headmaster's daughter?" She rubbed the sleep from her eyes again and yawned to wake herself up.

Lily grinned. "Yeah, that's my Silvy. She's a great kid, but she tends to get into trouble. So will you watch out for her?"

Kris hesitated. "Yeah, if you agree to do something for me."

Lily's smile faded. "You're going to say the Jake word. WTF? Listening to your summoning spells gives me a migraine."

148

"I just need to know what happened to him. Did you take your soul?" She put her hands on her hips. "If you hear my summoning spells, why don't you answer me?"

Lily shook her head. "There are rules. Just watch out for Silvy, okay?"

"Just tell me where he is!" Lily cried. "I need to know if he's alive."

"He's gone. That's all I can tell you." Lily then vanished in a whirl of smoke.

CHAPTER 3

Kris gulped down coffee the next morning. She didn't get much sleep, but felt wide awake and anxious to get started with her class. She kept replaying her conversation with Lily over in her mind.

Lily hadn't said Jake was dead, only gone. What did that mean? Was Jake dead or alive?

Students poured into her classroom. She scanned their faces and prayed she was ready for this. Hell, she was a decade older than them, so she should be able to handle a few teenagers. But she didn't spot Silvy among the newcomers.

Kris called out the register and noticed two girls were missing. Silvana Eldry and Melanie Greenwood. Great, Lily's kid had decided to bunk off from class.

She spotted one name she recognised: Tristen Thornwood. The fae prince.

The kid looked gorgeous and had a weird magnetic energy around him.

Typical male fae royal. She knew that from meeting the Unseelie King once before. And that man had power.

Kris started the class and went over what they'd be studying that day and for the rest of the term.

Once the class was over, Silvy came over to her. She had turned up a few minutes late with a note explaining why. "Miss Dixson, do you have any books on fae artefacts?"

"That's not part of the homework."

"No, it's not for class. It's something personal."

"I'll see what I can dig up."

"Thanks." Silvy turned to leave.

"Lily said to tell you, you're to stay out of trouble this term," Kris blurted out before she could stop herself.

Why had she said that? Lily wouldn't even tell her anything about Jake.

Silvy froze. "You saw Lily?" She furrowed her brow. "But she's a banshee."

"Technically, she's a reaper now. Lily always did like making her way through the ranks." Kris rolled her eyes. "She was my friend before she died. She talked about you a lot."

"Good, then she stopped the guy who killed her." Silvy smiled. "I thought she'd move on after that."

"Lilly won't let death stop her, believe me. Sorry to hear about your mum."

Silvy winced. "Thanks. Sorry for your loss too."

Kris gaped at her. "How do you know about that? Did your dad tell you?"

She scoffed at that. "My dad doesn't gossip. No, I can see the pain surrounding your aura. You lost someone you love."

Kris swallowed hard. "I don't know what happened to him."

Why had she said that?

"For what it's worth. I don't think he's dead." Silvy swung her bag over her shoulder.

"What? Where is he then?" Her heart lurched.

How could this girl know whether Jake was alive or not? She was a kid. Although she did have a pretty strong aura of power around her.

151

Silvy shrugged. "I read auras like my dad can. I'm not sure how it works."

"It's good to meet you, Silvy." Kris smiled. "I'll see can dig up anything about ancient artefacts."

A few weeks passed in a blur. Silvy stopped by again after class. Kris had enjoyed getting to know her and the other students.

She still kept hearing a wolf every night, and it drove her mad. What did it mean?

Silvy came in after class when she was in the middle of a spell. "Miss Dixon, can I ask you something?"

Kris ran a hand through her hair. "Sure, what's up?"

"Am I interrupting?" Silvy furrowed her brow.

"No." Kris sighed. "My spells never work anymore." She waved her hand and the candles extinguished.

"Were you trying to find your fiancé?"

Kris nodded and hung her head. "It never works. My spells never seem to do anything now." She ran a hand through her hair again. "Is my aura still broken?"

"Yeah. How did you lose your fiancé?"

"Lost is the right term. I still don't know what happened. What do you need help with?"

When she hadn't been teaching classes, she'd been busy researching leads about Jake. She needed a break, though.

"You're a witch who does spirit magic, right?" Silvy looked hopeful. Kris nodded again. "Can you come and help me with my mum?"

"Your mum died. Do you want me to summon her spirit?" She didn't know how to feel about that. If it brought the girl some closure, she supposed she could give it a try. But given how unreliable her magic had been recently, she didn't want to disappoint her.

"It's a lot more complicated than that. I'll take you to her." Silvy held out her hand.

Kris grasped her hand.

They reappeared in a large bedroom. A blond haired

woman lay in the bed, eyes closed, unmoving.

"This is my mum, Freya."

"I know. I met her a few times." Kris frowned. "Your dad said—"

Had Lucas lied to her? she wondered.

"Until recently we thought she died a few months ago. Maeve poisoned her and the king took her soul. That's why need your help," Silvy explained. "Can you help me summon her soul and put it back in her body?"

Kris gaped at her. "I—I don't know if I can." She touched Freya's forehead. "Her body is so weak. Even if I did manage it, I can't guarantee she'll survive."

She never expected Silvy to ask this of her. Nor had she ever attempted such potent magic. Such a thing was probably way beyond her abilities.

"Can you at least try?"

Kris hesitated. The king had a hell of a lot more power than her. "Silvy—"

"Your fiancé is still alive if that helps."

Her heart lurched. "How do you know that?" She had always known Jake wasn't dead and Lily had said as much. But she never had any real proof until now.

"People who love each other have links in their auras. Yours is still there, but it's broken and barely held together. Weird, I've never seen that before."

Kris closed her eyes for a moment. "You know where he is?"

Silvy shook her head. "My power has limits."

Kris took a deep breath. "I will try a spell." She placed her hands on Freya and chanted a spirit summoning spell. A cool breeze whipped through the room.

Glass shattered as a black wolf leapt in through the window.

Kris gasped and backed away. How had that thing followed her here? What did it even want?

"Oh goody, a Lycan," Silvy groaned. "Back off, wolf boy." Air rippled between her fingers.

The Lycan growled and advanced toward them.

Silvy glanced between Kris and the Lycan. "Holy crackers, I think that's your fiancé."

Kris gaped at her. "What? It can't be Jake."

"It's him. Your link in your aura is growing stronger."

"Jake?" Kris walked over to the wolf. "Is that you?"

The Lycan shifted into Jake. "Stop getting in the king's way," he growled, shifted back and leapt out the window.

That was it? That was all he had to say?

Kris gritted her teeth and shook her head to clear it, to make sure she wasn't dreaming.

"Stay with Freya." Large gossamer wings unfurled from Silvy's back. "I'll find out where he's going." She turned and flew out the window.

Kris stood there in stunned disbelief. She couldn't believe it. Jake was alive. He looked more or less as she remembered. Tall with a muscular build, long black hair and dark eyes. He still had a black sleeve tattoo covering his right arm. Yet he looked at her like he didn't even know her. So the wolf hadn't killed him after all. He had become the wolf. Or Lycan, as Silvy called it.

"What's going on?" The pink-haired healer came in. "I heard a crash."

Kris just stood there, unsure what to say or do. She felt numb inside.

"Are you alright?" The healer put a hand on her shoulder. "What happened?"

Kris shook her head again. "I'm not hurt. Silvy went after that thing. Goodness, I can't let anything happen to her." She felt stupid for not reacting sooner. Kris should be the one going after him, not Silvy.

Her father would go ballistic if he found out Kris had been with her when the Lycan attacked.

She walked to the window and when she went to climb out, a ward of energy blocked her.

"Damn it, Jake!" She gritted her teeth. She'd recognise his handiwork anywhere. He had put a ward up to prevent her running after him. The bastard!

How had Silvy managed to get through that? She knew she shouldn't be surprised. The girl was a lot more powerful than she appeared to be. She had felt that earlier when she cast the spell and something jolted between them.

"You should check on Freya," she told the healer. "Make sure she is okay." Kris paced up and down in front of the window, wondering what to do next.

The healer went over to Freya, then let out a cry of alarm as Freya's eyes flew open. Freya bolted up in the bed and stared at them, dazed.

Kris put a hand over her mouth. "Holy crap! How are you here?" She had only meant to cast a summoning spell to call her spirit. To give Silvy a chance to say goodbye. She had known deep down there was no way they could retrieve Freya's soul from the Unseelie King. "Freya, is that you?" Kris took a cautious step toward the bed.

Given how unpredictable her magic had been recently, she couldn't be sure Freya's spirit had come back. Perhaps something else had come through. Some other entity to possess the empty vessel of Freya's body. Hell, the king could have sent someone through for all she knew. He had enough power to do such a thing.

"Where is Silvy?" Freya seemed to say it more to herself than to them. She climbed out of bed and made her way across the room.

"Wait, you're not well enough to go anywhere." The healer put out a hand to stop her, but Freya ignored her and scrambled out the window. The ward flashed against her, but Freya pushed against it and finally got through.

Kris and the healer stared after her in disbelief.

"How is she awake?" The healer murmured. "Her body was dying. There's no way her soul could have come back."

A pit of dread formed in Kris' stomach. "I'm not sure that was Freya. It might be something else." She went to

155

the window, but Jake's barrier still blocked her. It would take time to get it down. One way or another, she had to figure out what the hell was going on.

Silvy, along with Freya and Tristen, finally came back an hour or so later. The healer got to work checking on Freya and they all headed back to Goodwin Castle.

Kris' nerves grew as she waited outside in the hallway. She told Silvy that Freya might not have come back and it could be something else. The girl didn't react well to that, but Kris supposed she couldn't blame her. She knew she'd be in deep trouble for this. Lucas would probably sack her on the spot for using such unsanctioned magic. Lucas arrived a while later and did indeed lecture her.

It had amazed Kris when Silvy had stepped in and ordered her father not to take Kris' job away. Kris still didn't understand what had happened. Somehow she suspected Silvy had been the one responsible. Maybe Kris' magic had just given her the right outlet. She didn't know why it happened. But that power had come from Silvy, not from her.

Later she returned to the academy, but she couldn't sleep, so she headed outside.

She didn't need to cast her senses out now to know Jake was nearby.

"You're not doing a very good job of masking your presence anymore," she murmured.

Jake appeared out of the shadows. "You need to stay away from that girl. She's nothing but trouble."

"That's it? That's all you have to say to me after months of being apart?" She put her hands on her hips. "What the hell happened to you? I loved you. We were supposed to get married. You just disappeared without even saying goodbye. For Christ's sake, why are you after that kid? She's just a girl."

"She's more than just a girl and you know it. She has something the king wants and he'll do everything in his power to get it." Jake gave her a grim look. "That's why

I'm here. The king turned me into a Lycan. I'm now one of his servants. That's why I couldn't come back. If I tried to, the king would use you against me and I couldn't let that happen."

"You could have told me the truth before now. You let me think you were dead!" She went to slap him but he caught hold of her hand.

"I do love you, Kris. That will never change, but we can't be together anymore. You should leave the academy too. This is not a safe place for anyone."

She gave a harsh laugh. "Why, what's your precious king going to do?"

"In case you hadn't noticed, the Ever Realm is falling apart. Soon it will disappear completely. That's why the king needs the power of the Everlight Stone to put everything back into balance. That's one of the reasons he turned me."

"You'd better not do anything to hurt that girl, Jake. She is one of my students and I'm rather fond of her."

Jake snorted. "If you want to help her, convince her to hand over the second half of the stone. Once the king gets what he wants, I'll be free and we can be together again."

Kris drew away. "What makes you think I'd accept you like this?" The words stung them both. She didn't care if he changed into a Lycan. That wouldn't change her feelings for him, but his recent actions might.

She couldn't be sure she could trust him anymore. Not while he worked for the Unseelie King at least.

"Accept me or don't. The king will get what he wants. Just back off and stay the hell out of his way." Jake shifted back into his wolf form and ran off into the night.

Kris finally let the tears fall and wondered if she would ever get back the man she had once loved.

EPILOGUE

A few months later Kris still couldn't believe everything that happened. Silvy turned out to be the one who possessed the power of the Everlight and had bound herself to Tristen. Now the Unseelie King was gone, and the Ever Realm was finally back in balance. Back to one whole realm, as it had once been.

She celebrated along with everyone else at the academy as the final term ended and the final year students graduated. Tristen and Silvy were now the king and queen of the fae. She still had trouble getting her head around that.

Despite the king being gone, she hadn't seen Jake again, yet. Or heard anything about him.

Silvy came up to her wearing her cap and gown for graduation. "Kris, I just wanted to thank you for your help this term. I couldn't have done this without you." Silvy wrapped her arms around her and hugged her.

Kris smiled and returned her hug. "I didn't do much. All of this was your doing, not mine."

"You helped to save my mother. I doubt I would have done that without you. So thank you." Silvy flashed her bright smile. "I have something else for you. There's someone here who wants to see you." She motioned behind them to where Jake stood, skulking in the shadows.

"He's still a Lycan. I can't change that, but I gave him an amulet so he can control when he turns. But he is free now."

Kris' heart lurched. She stood there for a moment just staring.

"Go and talk him," Silvy said. "No matter what happens, love doesn't really go away. I know that." She grinned as Tristen came over and put an arm around her.

Kris reluctantly went over to Jake. "Hi." She kept her eyes on the ground, unable to meet his gaze.

"Hi."

"Why haven't you been to see me before now?" she asked and finally looked up at him.

"I wasn't sure you'd want to see me," Jake admitted. "Not after everything that happened. I wouldn't blame you for that."

Kris hesitated, then wrapped her arms around him. "I can't say we can pick up where we left off. But don't we owe it to ourselves to give it another go? Feelings haven't changed."

Jake nodded and pulled her in for a kiss. "I'd like that."

If you enjoyed this book it would be great if you could leave a review. For more news about my books sign up for my newsletter on tiffanyshand.com/newsletter

ALSO BY TIFFANY SHAND

EXCALIBAR INVESTIGATIONS SERIES

Touched by Darkness Book 1

Bound to Darkness Book 2

Rising Darkness Book 3

Excalibar Investigations Complete Box Set

SHADOW WALKER SERIES

Shadow Walker

Shadow Spy

Shadow Sworn

Shadow Walker Complete Box Set

ANDOVIA CHRONICLES

Dark Deeds Prequel

The Calling

ROGUES OF MAGIC SERIES

Bound By Blood

Archdruid

Bound By Fire

Old Magic

Dark Deception

Sins Of The Past

Reign Of Darkness

Rogues Of Magic Complete Box Set Books 1-7

ROGUES OF MAGIC NOVELLAS

Wyvern's Curse

Forsaken

On Dangerous Tides

The Rogues of Magic Short Story Collection

EVERLIGHT ACADEMY TRILOGY

Everlight Academy, Book 1: Faeling

Everlight Academy Book 2: Fae Born

Everlight Academy Book 3: Fae Light

Everlight Tales Short Story Collection

THE AMARANTHINE CHRONICLES BOOK 1

Betrayed By Blood

Dark Revenge

The Final Battle

Fallen Avatar

The Arkadia Saga Complete Series

ABOUT THE AUTHOR

Tiffany Shand is a writing mentor, professionally trained copy editor and copy writer who has been writing stories for as long as she can remember. Born in East Anglia, Tiffany still lives in the area, constantly guarding her work space from the two cats which she shares her home with.

She began using her pets as a writing inspiration when she was a child, before moving on to write her first novel after successful completion of a creative writing course. Nowadays, Tiffany writes urban fantasy and paranormal romance, as well as nonfiction books for other writers, all available through eBook stores and on her own website.

Tiffany's favourite quote is *'writing is an exploration. You start from nothing and learn as you go'* and it is armed with this that she hopes to be able to help, inspire and mentor many more aspiring authors.

When she has time to unwind, Tiffany enjoys photography, reading, and watching endless box sets. She also loves to get out and visit the vast number of castles and historic houses that England has to offer.

Printed in Great Britain
by Amazon